FINAL
SPIN

Also by
Jocko Willink

FINAL SPIN

Jocko Willink

ST. MARTIN'S
PRESS
NEW YORK

First published in the United States by St. Martin's Press, an imprint of St. Martin's Publishing Group

FINAL SPIN. Copyright © 2021 by JOCKO COMMAND LLC. All rights reserved. Printed in the United States of America. For information, address St. Martin's Publishing Group, 120 Broadway, New York, NY 10271.

www.stmartins.com

Designed by Steven Seighman

The Library of Congress Cataloging-in-Publication Data is available upon request.

ISBN 978-1-250-27685-8 (hardcover)
ISBN 978-1-250-28016-9 (international, sold outside the U.S., subject to rights availability)
ISBN 978-1-250-27686-5 (ebook)

Our books may be purchased in bulk for promotional, educational, or business use. Please contact your local bookseller or the Macmillan Corporate and Premium Sales Department at 1-800-221-7945, extension 5442, or by email at MacmillanSpecialMarkets@macmillan.com.

First U.S. Edition: 2021
First International Edition: 2021

10 9 8 7 6 5 4 3 2 1

For Jeff Lang

1

How did I end up here? I'm smart. I'm funny.
I look pretty damn handsome if I do say so
myself.

But here I am.

Nowhere.

And it seems this is where I will always
be: nowhere.

Bedroom.

    It is not an apartment, but it looks
    like one.

        Cheap furniture.

            Well-used carpet.

                Not clean, but not
                dirty.

The bedroom is not unique in its wares.
Bed. Desk. Chair. Dresser. Small bedside table
with lamp. Overhead light. Janky ceiling fan,
spinning at a low speed.

Then there is the décor. Pictures hung

neatly on the walls. They are strange. Or at least indicate a strangeness that is hard to interpret. Harmless, but different.

Johnny walks in.
    Twentysomething.
        Leaning toward twenty.

Pretty damn handsome for an unkempt young man who stays up too late and eats the wrong foods and drinks more beer and whiskey than he should.

He looks at his brother.
    Johnny is frustrated.
        He tries to remain restrained, but it can be hard after all these years.

"What the hell, Cleaner? Man, I told you about these shirts." Arty looks distraught. Johnny sees. Johnny cannot stay frustrated. After all, this is Arty, his brother. And no one could really be mad at Arty.

"What? Is it not clean?" Arty replies, earnestly concerned, wondering if he has somehow failed his brother.

"No, Arty. It isn't that it's not clean. It's clean. But it's just a T-shirt . . ."

"I know," Arty cuts in. "It's a hundred-percent cotton T-shirt. I used a warm-warm cycle. It shouldn't have shrunk at all. I'm always careful about that."

"It's not shrunk, Arty. That's not it. It's . . . just . . . never mind. Forget it."

"Forget what, Johnny? What's wrong?" This is killing Arty. The one thing he was supposed to be good at. And it seems like he messed it up.

"Arty," Johnny replies as kindly as he can, "it's just that . . . it's a T-shirt. You don't press T-shirts. You don't put starch in T-shirts, buddy."

"But the creases are sharp, aren't they?" Arty replies, wondering what on earth the problem could be.

"The creases are sharp," Johnny concedes, "but that's not the point. You don't put military creases in T-shirts. I've told you this before, Arty."

"But why? Cotton holds the starch really well."

Johnny starts to get frustrated again. He's been down this road before.

Many, many times.

"Look, Cleaner, I know that. You always tell me that. And I always tell you: You just don't starch and press T-shirts because . . . because you just don't do it."

"Mom likes hers pressed."

Johnny lets out a sigh.

Arty realizes he's gone too far.

"Listen, Arty, I get it. But I'm not Mom. And I don't want my T-shirts to be starched and pressed. It's a Black Sabbath T-shirt! I just wear it out with a pair of jeans, okay? Can you just give them a simple wash and dry from now on? Please?"

"Low heat, tumble dry?" Arty asks, wanting to get a good procedure locked down.

Johnny smiles. "Yeah, Arty. I think that would be perfect. Thanks, bud."

"I can do it now," Arty offers.

"I have to go."

"Okay. It won't happen again, Johnny."

"Thanks, Arty," Johnny says with a gentle smile.

"And Johnny?" Arty asks.

"What?"

"I'm sorry."

"It's okay, bud. It's okay."

Johnny feels a little bad as Arty walks away.

They are brothers--they even look a little alike--it isn't too much of a stretch to see the similar genes. Dark hair. Blue eyes. Pronounced eyebrows. But that is where the similarities end.

After all, Arty is: different.
A little pudgy.
Glasses.

It is possible to tell from looking at his face that something isn't quite right. There are medical names that could be assigned, but most of those wouldn't quite hit the mark. He is older than Johnny by six years. But his peculiarities keep him living at home.

Johnny, on the other hand, doesn't have an excuse to still be living at home--other than Arty and his mom. They both need him around.

That's what he tells himself, anyway.

Johnny's bedroom is the same room he has always had. Mattress on the floor. No box spring. No bed frame. Posters of rock bands on the wall from when he was younger. Black Sabbath. Motörhead. Led Zeppelin. AC/DC. Some muscle cars too. He hadn't bothered to take them down as he outgrew them. He also hadn't bothered to clean his room very often. Clothes, remnants of food, and beer cans on the floor.

This is all a stark contrast to Arty's room: clinically clean with the bed tightly made.

And then there are the walls of Arty's room and their curious décor. The walls neatly display pictures of clothes, washing machines, and dryers. There are brochures about various lines of laundry equipment on his little desk. Some of the more colorful ones are also hanging on the wall. There are also coupons for laundry detergents, fabric softeners, and stain removal products on the desk in an envelope.

The source of his nickname, "Cleaner," is no mystery at all.

Arty likes to clean.
Laundry, to be exact.

2

This is it, I guess.
This is as good as it is going to get.
Where did I go wrong?
Where was the misstep?
Was it one? Or was it many? A thousand little errors landing me here.
Landing me nowhere. Nowhere but here.

"Nice shirt, man," Goat says with a smile as he sees Johnny's starched Black Sabbath T-shirt, its military creases running from each shoulder down to the waist.

"Up yours," Johnny replies.

"That cotton really holds the crease, doesn't it?"

"Yeah it does," Johnny says.

"You couldn't iron them out or anything?"

"I tried, but damn. He uses an industrial press. And he looks at me like I'm ripping his heart out. What can I say? My brother is crazy."

"Yeah, but that son-of-a-bitch can iron some shirts, can't he?"

"He sure as hell can. You want another one?"

"What time do we have to be at work?" Goat asked.

"Not until ten thirty."

"Sheeeit. Let's do this."

"Two more, Lucy," Johnny says to the barmaid.

BB's Bar.
    Dingy working-class watering hole.
        Cheap vinyl seats.
            Even cheaper drinks.

Goat is about the same age as Johnny, though he looks a little younger. His dark skin has an almost childlike texture. His black hair looks as if it is always organized, regardless of what he has been doing. His eyes are dark and deep. He is handsome. He too has that look about him that says he shouldn't be here.

Shouldn't be in a dead-end job.

Shouldn't be in a dead-end bar.

Shouldn't be in a dead-end life.

But he is.

8

FINAL SPIN

Arty enters the bar.

He is not comfortable in this place.

Dirty. Dark. Bad smells.

He tries to think of other things that smell good:

> Fabric softener.
> > Lemon detergent.
> > > A clean load of linens.

But this place does not smell those ways. It smells other ways.

> Beer.
> > Smoke.
> > > Grease.

Arty sees Johnny and Goat and makes his way over to them.

"What's up, Arty?" Johnny asks.

"Hi, Johnny. Hi, Goat," Arty responds.

"How's it going, Cleaner?" Goat asks.

"Good. Fine. I mean good," Arty says nervously.

"What are you doing here?" Johnny asks. "Is everything all right?"

"Everything is fine. Good. But. I . . .

I brought you this shirt. No starch. No creases. The way you like it."

Arty hands Johnny a nicely folded T-shirt. Johnny takes it and holds it up. It unfurls as he does, revealing a Motörhead logo. Johnny smiles and nods.

"It's perfect, Arty. Perfect. Thanks."

"No problem. I'm sorry about that one," Arty replies, pointing to the starched Black Sabbath shirt Johnny is wearing.

"Ah . . . don't worry about this. It's cool. You want a Coke or something?"

"No. I can't. I've got to get back to the laundromat. I'm checking dryer temperatures."

"You sure? Just one Coke?"

"I'm sure. I want to check the temperatures at their peak. About fifteen minutes from now," Arty says, looking at his calculator watch.

"Fair enough. Well, thanks for the new shirt. I'll put it on before work."

"You're welcome. You're welcome. See you later. Bye, Goat." Arty steps back and walks away.

"Later, Cleaner," Johnny says loudly.

"Later!" Goat adds.

Arty makes his way past a group of men.

FINAL SPIN

Working men. Approaching thirty. They have some drinks in them.

They also have some kind of attitude.
Some kind of anger that needs a target.
Arty makes a good target.

"Hey!" one of them yells. It's a loud yell. Loud enough to stop Arty. Also loud enough to draw the attention of Johnny and Goat. Arty looks at the rowdy man.

The man smiles and shouts:

"Nice fucking outfit!"

His friends burst into laughter.
Arty is startled.
Confused.
He looks down at his brown corduroy pants.
Checks the sleeves of his brown turtleneck.
He doesn't understand.
He looks up toward the door.
He is frozen for a second, but finally builds up the courage and composure to start walking. Quickly. Toward the door.
He makes it out.

"What a fucking retard!" the man shouts.
His friends laugh.

Johnny does not.

Instead, he exhales deeply. Then tilts his head.

"Gonna be one of those nights," he says quietly to Goat.

"Indeed," Goat replies.
Goat and Johnny stop drinking.

They have a new mission.

They watch the loudmouth.
He keeps drinking.
Some of his friends leave.

Finally, it is just him, one other guy, and two young ladies drinking and carrying on.

The group decides it is time to leave.
Cash placed on table.
Drinks finished.
They head for the door.
Johnny and Goat follow.

The group spills out onto the sidewalk. They are drunker than Johnny and Goat thought. The group heads down the sidewalk, west toward the main strip.

Johnny and Goat know where they are heading: another bar, a few doors down. They can't let the group get too close. Johnny and Goat close the distance to within a few feet.

"Hey!" Johnny shouts in a hostile, violent tone.

But the group does not sense that violence. They slowly turn around.

Johnny looks at the loudmouth and growls, "Nice fucking outfit."

The man has long since forgotten his earlier comments. But knows something is amiss.

"What's your fucking prob--" he begins to ask in a menacing tone that would scare off most would-be attackers.

But his question is cut short by an over-hand right from Johnny that connects squarely with the rowdy's jaw.

He goes down.

At the same time, Goat tackles the other drunk to the ground and starts punching.

The girls back away.

They want no part of this scene.

Johnny follows his opponent to the ground and lands three more punches to his face. Then he grabs him by the throat and squeezes. The man is horrified.

"You like picking on people?" Johnny says.

"What?" the man says/chokes as he gasps for air.

"I said, 'Do you like picking on people?'"

"No. I don't . . . I just . . . no."

"You remember that retard? With the funny clothes?" The drunk is shocked. "That was my brother."

"Oh. I'm . . . I didn't . . . I mean . . ."

"Who's the retard now, you piece of shit?"

"I'm sorry . . . I'm sorry . . ." The man gurgles as his airway is compressed.

Johnny relaxes his grip on the man's neck.

"You need to think about what you say to people. Understand?"

The man nods.

"UNDERSTAND?" Johnny asks again, demanding an answer.

"Yes, yes."

"Say it," Johnny orders. "Say you understand."

"I understand," the horrified man replies. "I understand."

"Good," Johnny says as he regains his composure, gets off the man, and stands up. Goat does the same.

"Good evening, ladies," he says.

Johnny and Goat turn and walk away.

Adrenaline subsides. Goat looks at his watch.

"Just in time for work," he says to Johnny.

Johnny looks at his watch. 10:22 P.M.

"Indeed. Just in time."

3

Who was I fighting?
   Defending my brother?
   Really?
   Them?
   Or am I fighting me?
   I look around and the world seems to be
passing me by. I mean: I'm here. I'm in it.
But I'm not part of it. I'm only a bit part.
Counting time. Stacking boxes. Part of the
machine.

"You would think Americans survived on fucking
mayonnaise," Goat says, disgusted.
   "No shit."

   Stock boys.
      Boxes.
         Tile floor and industrial shelves.
            Food.
               Detergent.
                  Electronics.

Pretty much anything can be found here. Every day, from the time the doors open until they close, there are customers here. Buying milk and batteries and toilet paper and garbage bags.

Tomatoes.
   Popcorn.
      Salami.

People can buy anything here. And they do. Consumption in massive quantities to fill their massive bellies and run up their massive credit card debt.

   People: flesh-covered robot beings in need of fuel and meaning.

   They find both here.

"I mean honestly--who the fuck needs a half gallon of Miracle Whip for their house?" Goat asks, earnestly trying to comprehend this madness.
   "Well, obviously a bunch of people need it. All this will be gone in a couple of days."
   Goat shakes his head. "What the hell do

they do? Put it in their cereal or something?"

"I think they butter up their wives with it."

"Goddamn. That's fucking disgusting."

"Yeah it is," Johnny agrees.

From the end of the aisle, a loud, high-pitched voice breaks their conversation. Gerry, the night manager. "You guys need to stop talking and get that stuff stacked up! Less talking and more stocking! We've still got pickles, mustard, Crisco, and canned ham!"

"I got your canned ham," Goat whispers under his breath.

Gerry walks toward Goat and Johnny.

Thin.
    Late thirties.
        Smoker.
            Greasy hair.
                Beige Levi Dockers.
                    Polo shirt:
                    Yellow.

Gold-colored necklace, with cross.
    Gold-colored watch:
        Fake.

"What did you say?" Gerry asks aggressively.

Goat stands up straight and belts out, "I said, 'I got your canned ham.'"

Gerry shakes his head. He tries to think of an original comeback, but he can't think of anything good. He resorts to all he knows. "Well, you just keep running your mouth like that and we'll see if you ever make supervisor." Not wanting to engage in a verbal battle, Gerry quickly walks away.

Goat stands there, shaking his head. "Motherfucker," he says quietly, then, unable to contain himself, shouts, "Supervise this, you weasel-looking motherfucker!"

Johnny looks at him. "I'd fucking kill myself if I ever made supervisor at this shithole."

"Yeah, and that prick walking around like he's fucking Steve Jobs."

"Loser."

"Fucking loser."

"At least he's easy to rip off," Johnny concedes.

"Yeah, he's got that going for him. I'm getting a couple bottles of Jack tonight," Goat says.

"I'm getting the nastiest rotgut gin I can find."

"Wine is fine, but whiskey is quicker . . ." Goat sings "Suicide Solution" by Ozzy Osbourne.

"And I'm getting a nice big bottle of Perfecto for Arty."

"He's using Perfecto now? What happened to Everfresh?"

"Some new and improved Perfecto formula he read about. It's got crystals in it apparently."

"Crystals?" Goat asks.

"Yeah. You know. Some kind of brightening bullshit. Redder reds and bluer blues . . ."

"Let's get him some more of that Eternal Spring fabric softener too. That shit was legit. I was feeling like fucking James Brown with that shit!"

"Hell yes. Eternal Spring--coming at you . . ."

4

He finds happiness here.
Where is mine?
Ignorance is bliss, they say.
He makes me think maybe they are right.
Because he finds bliss. Here. Of all places.
Here.

"Hi, Johnny," Arty says with a giant smile on his face.

"What's up, Cleaner? I brought you some presents."

Johnny places a massive bottle of Perfecto laundry detergent and a box of Eternal Spring fabric softener on the counter Arty is standing near. Behind him and his counter is the dry-cleaning portion of the laundromat. On the wall there is a sign. It reads:

'DE WASSERETTE'

LAUNDROMAT

It is a standard laundromat.
   Industrial presses.
      Irons.
         Giant washing machines and dryers.

Things are worn out, but clean and organized.

Freshly pressed clothes in thin, clear plastic bags hang from a conveyor belt that disappears toward the back. In front of the counter, the side where Johnny stands, are coin-operated washing machines and dryers.

"The new Perfecto!" Arty says as he lifts the bottle and begins reading, "'All-new dual-action crystals clean and brighten.' This stuff sounds awesome."

"Don't forget about that Eternal Spring there," Johnny says.

"I won't forget. That stuff is the best for heavy denims," Arty explains, nodding with a smile on his face.

"What do you have going on today?" Johnny asks.

"Well, I did lint this morning. Collected coins from the washers. I've got two loads of darks, one load of lights, and one cold-cold. Then I'll help Mrs. Vossen with the pressing.

We've got a bunch. Everything. Suits. Dresses. Uniforms. It's going to be really good. Is that stuff yours?" Arty says as he points to a bag of laundry Johnny is holding.

"Nah. This is Goat's. I said you could take care of it for him."

"For sure! No problem at all. Any special items?"

"No, Arty. There's no special items. It's just clothes. Plain old clothes."

"Well . . . any special instructions?"

"Yeah. No starch. No creases. But plenty of Eternal Spring. Goat says that stuff makes him feel like James Brown."

"I don't know," Arty says, looking concerned. "I think James Brown wore mostly synthetics. Eternal Spring works best with natural fibers."

"Well. It makes Goat feel good."

"Okay. I'll make sure. No starch, no creases, extra Eternal Spring."

"Perfect."

Mrs. Vossen, a Dutch woman in her early sixties, approaches from the back of the building.

Short.
Wrinkled.

> Plain, utilitarian gray hair: shoulder length.

She says something to Johnny in Dutch and begins laughing.

Arty chuckles too.

"What'd she say?" Johnny asks.

"She says your clothes always look cleaner than you do."

Johnny gives her a look and shakes his head and then says to no one in particular, "Well, that's just the way things go, I guess."

Mrs. Vossen begins shaking her head too and speaking more Dutch. Arty responds to her, also in Dutch. She gives Johnny another dirty look and then says something very pointed in Dutch. Johnny looks at Arty. Arty translates again: "She wants to know why you still work in that store."

"Because they pay me," Johnny responds.

Arty translates back into Dutch. Mrs. Vossen does not like this answer. She responds sharply, wagging her finger at Johnny. Arty delivers the message. "She says you are too smart and too handsome to stack boxes."

Johnny ponders that statement. *She's right,* he thinks to himself. He smiles lightly, then says, "Tell her to tell that to the rest of the world."

Arty turns to Mrs. Vossen and speaks more Dutch.

Mrs. Vossen laughs loudly and shakes her head. She walks away, toward the machines out back.

Johnny watches her. He tilts his head like he doesn't understand the meaning of her behavior--like he doesn't know what she thinks of him.

But he does.

Yes.

He does.

He turns to Arty. "Listen, buddy, I've got to get going."

"Where?"

"You know. Work and stuff."

"Okay. Well, thanks for the Perfecto and the Eternal Spring. And tell Goat his clothes will be ready in about two hours and twelve minutes."

"Two hours and twelve minutes?"

"Yeah. That is with extra rinse time. It adds nine minutes."

"I'll tell him, Arty. Thanks, bud."

"Okay. Bye."

"See you later."

5

Too smart and too handsome.
   But here I am.
   Stacking boxes.

"You know what," Goat blurts out, "I've had a couple of corn dogs in my time. But a box of forty-eight? What the fuck is that?"

"Yeah," Johnny agrees. "You've got to be one twisted motherfucker to buy a box of forty-eight fucking corn dogs."

"And it says they're microwavable. You know what that means: Soggy on one side. Still a little cold in the middle. We are talking nasty."

"I will say this though, at nine ninety-nine a box, they are affordable."

"That's like, what . . . twenty cents apiece?"

"Yep. You got to admit, that's a pretty good deal."

Their conversation is interrupted by a

shout from Gerry at the end of the aisle, "Less talking and more stocking!"

"Speaking of corn dogs," Goat mutters under his breath.

"You guys are taking way too long to get that stuff stocked up. Way too long!" Gerry continues.

Goat takes another shot at Gerry under his breath. "How would you like one of these things stocked up your ass, you weasel-looking motherfucker."

Gerry shakes his head. Finally, he shouts, "If you guys don't learn to work faster, you'll never move up to management. You'll be stock boys for the rest of your lives." He turns and walks away. But his statement remains. Johnny and Goat work silently for a few minutes.

Finally Johnny says, "I'm not going to be a fucking stock boy for the rest of my life."

"What?" Goat asks. "You want to get promoted or something?"

"No, man. I'm not going to get promoted. But I'm not doing this shit forever. What kind of life is this?"

"Free whiskey," Goat jokes.

Johnny isn't joking.

"Yeah, free whiskey, but fuck this. What even is this? Is this the way we're supposed to go through life? Working for shit? Stacking fucking corn dogs? No, man. I'm not going to do it."

"Well, what are you going to do then? What even can you do?"

"I don't know, man. But something. Something . . ."

They go quiet.

In silence, it just becomes the boxes.

The tile.

The fluorescent lights.

The industrial shelves.

It is a minimum-wage job.

It is a Maxi-Mart polo shirt.

It is gallons of mayonnaise and giant cans of beans and corn dogs.

And.

For Johnny:

It is life.

6

Is this really it?
  This?
  What about her?

She is a pretty but tough-looking girl. Thick,
black hair that wants to curl, but is for the most
part straightened by its own weight and volume.

      Pale skin.

            Dark eyes.

                  Eyes with a hint of fight
                  left in them.

                  But most of the fight
                  is gone.

Worn away by long hours and hard work and
worn away by the reality of life.

           Jessica.

"Where have you been?" she asks.

"Working. Where else?" Johnny responds defensively.

"So you can't call or anything?"

"Sorry. I'm a prick."

"Yeah, you are."

"You've never held that against me before--don't start now . . ."

"You buy me a drink and I'll forgive you."

"Lucy! SoCo and Coke!" Johnny shouts to the barmaid.

"SoCo and Coke. Got it," the bartender responds.

"How's work?" Johnny asks, although he knows the answer.

"The usual. Mark's an asshole. Everybody that comes into that place is a fucking asshole. And I do what I do: Smile and kiss their ass."

"Why don't you quit?" Johnny asks. It's an earnest question, even though the answer is known by him.

She knows the answer too.

She also has the same question:

"Why don't you quit your fucking job, stock boy?"

"Ouch. Thanks."

"Well? I mean, fuck. Of course I'd quit that job, same as you. But who's gonna pay the rent?"

The bartender approaches them and places the Southern Comfort and Coke in front of Jessica. "SoCo and Coke," she says, matter-of-fact.

"Thanks, Lucy," Johnny tells her.

"Thanks, Johnny," Jessica says to Johnny.

"Anything for you, darlin'," he says with a smile.

"Great. You're horny."

"Hey," he replies defensively, "I'm just--"

"Don't worry. I am too," she says with a smile.

7

She looks beautiful.
    Why is she here? In bed? With me?
    How did she end up here?
    This is no place for a girl like her.

With that hair.

        Those eyes.

            That skin.

She should be married to a banker somewhere.
    Living in a mansion.

                What is this life?

Her eyes slowly open.
    Johnny is staring at her.
    Not awkwardly. But with intent.
    She looks at her wrist for a watch. It isn't
there.

She grabs his wrist and pulls his watch into her view.

"Fuck," she says.

"What?"

"I'm fucking late."

"Late for what?"

"For work!"

"Fuck work."

Jessica gets out of bed.

He studies her body and confirms:

She is beautiful.

She scans the floor, obviously looking for something.

"Where the fuck are my clothes?" she asks.

"They're on the floor."

"No, they're not on the floor," she says, frustrated.

"You're beautiful."

"Thanks. But where are my fucking clothes?"

"They're not on the floor?"

"NO! I've got to go. What the fuck?"

"They're gone."

"What? Where?"

"My brother. You know, Arty. The Cleaner. He took them to the laundromat. He takes my clothes every morning. He took yours too. That's what he does."

Jessica shakes her head. "Shit. Let me borrow some shorts or something."

"Shorts: third drawer down. T-shirts: second drawer down."

Jessica opens the drawers and there they are.

Clean.
    Folded.
        Stacked perfectly.

She smiles.

"I wish I had a brother like this."

"It's got its benefits," Johnny says, chuckling, "I've never done a load of laundry myself in my life. I wouldn't even know how to."

"All my brother ever did for me was get me stoned when I was eleven."

"So having a brother that's a dealer has benefits as well, I guess."

"Yeah. Until they get locked up," Jessica says as she pulls on the T-shirt, which comes down to her midthighs, like a short dress. "No need for shorts, I guess."

"Thanks," she says.

"No problem. I'll grab it back from you at some point."

"Not for the clothes, dummy."

Johnny smiles. "No problem at all . . ."

Jessica walks out the door.

She's like an angel.

A damn angel.

8

Johnny walks into the laundromat.

Arty sees him.

"Hi, Johnny," he says, excited to see his brother.

"What's up, Arty?" Johnny replies.

"Four singles on final spin and two of the front loaders on a heavy-cycle rinse."

"Sounds like a good morning."

"It is. It is," Arty replies, then continues somewhat nervously, "I used the new Perfecto yesterday. The stuff with the crystals."

"Oh yeah? Cool. How'd it work?"

"It was good. I mean . . . it was . . . um . . ."

"What is it, Arty?"

"Well, don't be mad, but I couldn't see that the crystals made that much of a difference. I mean, thanks so much for buying it for me and everything, but the crystals, they just weren't as good as I thought they would be."

Johnny smiles. He looks at Arty and thinks for a moment. "Nothing is ever as good as you think it is going to be, Arty. That's just the way life is. Nothing is ever perfect. Not even Perfecto--"

"Oh no, Johnny," Arty interrupts, "look at that over there. The Neptuna series seven commercial front triple loader with extra-large capacity, three rinse cycles, and a 330 RPM final spin. Look at it. Look how beautiful it is. I can watch it all day. That is perfect."

Johnny smiles.

That is happiness.
  Arty has it.
  I might not have it.
  I might not ever have it.
  But that is happiness.

"You're right, Arty. It is perfect. Absolutely."

Arty smiles as Mrs. Vossen approaches from the back of the laundromat. She speaks some Dutch to Arty. Arty translates for Johnny, "Mrs. Vossen says Mr. Vossen wants to talk to you in the back alone."

"Tell her fine, I'll follow her back."

Arty speaks and Mrs. Vossen turns and walks toward the back of the laundromat. Johnny follows. Past the industrial washing and pressing machines. Clothes on hangers. Pipes.

Office.

> Mr. Vossen's office.
>> The nucleus of the business.
>>> Desk.
>>>> Filing cabinets.
>>>>> Coffee machine.
>>>>>> Papers.
>>>>>>> Lots of papers.

Mr. Vossen is sitting at his desk. He looks up. Johnny speaks: "How are you doing, Mr. Vossen?"

Mr. Vossen gets right down to business. "I have a very important need to talk with you."

"Well, here I am. Shoot."

Mr. Vossen looks hard at Johnny. He doesn't know how to say it, which keeps him silent for an extra couple of seconds as he stares at Johnny. Then he just says it, "I am going to have to sell the laundromat."

Johnny instantly knows what this means. He is flustered. "What? Wait. Why?"

"Well, I need money very badly."

"But once you sell this place, you won't have any income. Then what will you do? How will you eat?"

"I am going back to Holland. My brother has

a small restaurant there. It has fallen on hard times. He needs money and help getting the restaurant back on its feet."

"You're too old to get into the restaurant business. It's hard work."

"My brother and I can do it together."

"But still. It's a restaurant. They go out of business all the time."

"Some of them do. But some of them do well. This one can. But it needs some work. Some more seating outside. Some improvements to the décor. Maybe some new items on the menu. With some investments in the right things, it could really become something."

"How much money do you need to invest?"

"All told, about forty thousand."

"What about Mrs. Vossen? Doesn't she like living here?" Johnny asks.

Mr. Vossen shakes his head. "Thirty-five years here and she still doesn't even like to speak English. She wants to go home too."

"Your mind is made up, huh."

"I'm sorry, Johnny."

"And you need forty thousand dollars."

"Yes," Mr. Vossen replies sympathetically. "This is why I have to sell the laundromat. I'm telling you because I don't want to tell your brother. I can't. He loves this place so much. And he has been great help for many, many years. I know this place makes him very happy. But I must go. I feel bad to leave him like this."

"This place is his whole life," Johnny says as he shakes his head.

"I know. I'm very sorry. But I have no choice. I have to sell it. I have family to take care of too." Mr. Vossen sits quietly for a moment, then asks, "Will you tell your brother for me?"

Johnny nods. "I will. I'll tell him. But give me a couple of days."

"Okay. You come and tell me when you tell him so I can put an advertisement in the paper, okay?"

"I will, Mr. Vossen. I will let you know."

Johnny walks to the front of the laundromat. Mrs. Vossen looks at him with concern. Arty does not notice. He is holding a bag of laundry. As he hands it to Johnny, he speaks, "Here are your clothes."

"Thanks, Ar--" Johnny starts to reply before being cut off by Arty.

"I got the stain out of your gray sweatshirt with some Eliminator Plus stain remover. Your friend's clothes, the girl's, are in there too. They smelled nice even before I washed them. Really nice."

Johnny smiles and nods. "Yeah, Arty. She smells good. But listen, I have to get going. I'll see you at home, okay?"

"Okay."

Johnny lifts the bag a little bit. "And thanks for these. I appreciate it, Cleaner," he says.

Johnny walks toward the door.

Damn.

    Damn.

        Damn.

9

Damn.

Damn.

Damn.

"Yep. His whole world. Gone," Johnny explains to Goat and Dave.

Back at BB's Bar.

It's a table night.

Beers.

Dave is a fresh-faced kid. Twenty-one.

Goat finishes a sip and finally responds, "Whoever buys the place might keep it as a laundromat."

"I doubt it. That building is good real estate. Good location. I mean, they're going to do something with it. And even if they do keep it as a laundromat, it's not like they are going to let Arty work there like he does now. They'll clean it up, put in more coin-operated washers and dryers. A detergent vending machine. Arty won't have a job. And even if they keep him there, they'll just screw him over."

Goat nods.

"Fuck," Dave chimes in. "When are they selling it?"

"Soon. Mr. Vossen wants me to tell Arty so he can advertise it. Put up a 'FOR SALE' sign. All that shit."

"Man. Cleaner is going to lose it," Goat says with a sigh.

"Yeah he is. The simplest guy in the world with the simplest pleasure in life and he's going to get it snatched away," Johnny says as his anger starts to seep out.

"Maybe he can find another job. A different one," Dave suggests.

This suggestion frustrates Johnny even more and he responds, "That's the fucking point, Dave. He won't find a different job. That place is the only thing he knows. The only thing he wants to know." He thinks for a few moments before concluding, "If that place goes away, I don't know what will happen to him. But it won't be good."

"Fuck," Goat says dejectedly, "let's get one more and get out of here."

"You guys working tonight?" Dave asks.

"No, we're going to go watch an after-school special, idiot," Johnny says. "Lucy, three more, please."

10

He never deserved this.
What is wrong with this world?
Why is this happening to him?
The only pure soul in the world.
Punished.
For what?
Who does this?
Why?

Johnny and Goat stack oversized boxes of oversized bags of mixed nuts onto an oversized shelf.

Johnny, frustrated: "That's what's fucked up. When Arty is there, he is the happiest motherfucker in the world. Now he is going to be fucked. He will be miserable."

"Yeah," Goat replies, looking at Johnny. "But what the fuck can we do about it?"

Johnny shakes his head. "I don't know, man. I don't know."

Gerry rounds the corner of the aisle and sees them talking.

"Why are you guys talking and not stock-ing?"

"'Cause stocking SUCKS!" Goat replies.

"Well, you better get used to it, because you two are going to be doing it for a long time."

"What the fuck are you talking about?" Johnny says.

"I'm talking about neither one of you ever getting promoted," Gerry replies. "Anyway. Get busy. You guys need to have these nuts in place by the time I get done with the cash transfer." Gerry turns and walks away, around the corner toward the next aisle.

"I'll place these nuts right in your mouth, ya fuckin' weasel," Goat mutters.

More boxes stacked.

"Can you believe a piece of shit like that basically runs our lives?" Johnny asks.

"Don't remind me."

More boxes stacked, in silence.

Finally, Johnny breaks the quietness. "How much money do you think they have in that safe for the Wednesday transfer?"

"Fuck, man. A lot. Couple hundred thousand, I would think."

"A couple hundred thousand? Really?"

"Well, you've got a week's worth of cash

sitting in there. You know how much money people spend in this fucking place. It's ridiculous. Who knows--it might be more than a couple hundred thousand. Maybe even half a million," Goat says.

"A half a million," Johnny repeats, shaking his head, "and we get six seventy-five an hour."

"That and free whiskey," Goat says quickly. "And free laundry detergent too."

Johnny is now shaking his head. "Six seventy-five an hour."

Johnny loads three more boxes of nuts on the shelf. Then he stops.

He looks at Goat.

His face looks strained, but determined.

More determined than Goat has ever seen Johnny look.

"You know what?" Johnny asks. Goat doesn't have time to respond. "I'll tell you what. Fuck this place. It's time to go big."

"Big?" Goat asks, no idea what Johnny is talking about.

"Yeah, man," Johnny replies. "Fuck this place. Let's go big."

"How big are you talking?" Goat asks.

"Half a million big. We take what we deserve."

Goat lets loose a quiet chuckle as he recognizes what Johnny is saying--to steal the money from Maxi-Mart. He tries to cool down Johnny: "Yeah, that's going big. But it's a nonstarter, man."

"Why's that?" Johnny aggressively responds.

"First of all, they'd probably catch us in the act. We aren't robbers. And even if they didn't catch us--we'd have to live on the run-- and I ain't living on the run."

"Why not run away from this shit job . . . and this shithole town?"

"But we'd have to keep running. We wouldn't even be able to spend all that money or we'd get caught."

"We don't need to spend all the money. We just need forty thousand dollars."

"What?" Goat asks, not following Johnny's line of thinking at all.

"Forty thousand. That's all we need."

"For what?"

"For Mr. and Mrs. Vossen. That buys their laundromat--"

"You're fucking crazy."

Johnny is now dead serious. "No. You're fucking crazy if you want to stay here the rest of your life stacking fucking mixed nuts. Look at us. We got nothing. We are nothing.

Nothing but a chance to help my brother. A chance to do something worthwhile." He lets that sink in before continuing. "Or we can keep stocking shelves until we fucking die."

"You really think we could pull it off?" Goat asks, suddenly finding himself asking a serious question about a preposterous idea.

Johnny is already convinced. "Outsmart the Weasel? Are you kidding me? Of course we can pull it off. At a minimum, we can get the forty K for the Vossens. And maybe we get caught. Who fucking knows? But I'm ready to take some fucking chances."

Goat looks at Johnny. He's still not 100 percent sure if Johnny is serious. But he appreciates the enthusiasm and wants to support his buddy. Finally, he nods his head. "Fuck it then. I'm in."

Johnny smiles. "That's what I'm talking about. Fuck it."

11

Maybe I am crazy.
  To think something like this.
  To do something like this.
  Or.
  Maybe I'd be crazy not to.

"It's pretty straightforward, right?" Goat asks.

"We'll see," Johnny responds. Even though it is his idea, he is smart enough not to be cocky about it. Johnny is lying on his bed. Looking at the ceiling. He is thinking as he talks.

Goat is sitting in a chair, looking at Johnny, wondering. Wondering what the hell they are talking about. Wondering if he should play along with this game. Wondering where it all ends and wondering if that ending is better than the current ending he can foresee. Finally he asks, "How would we do it? I mean, what is the plan?"

"Well. We know this much. We need to get into the safe, right?"

"No shit," Goat says.

"Well, you're not a safecracker. Neither am I."

"No shit."

"But I know someone that can get that safe open," Johnny says with a smile.

Goat looks puzzled, almost as if perhaps Johnny has been leading a double life.

"Who?"

"The Weasel," Johnny says confidently.

"The Weasel?"

"Damn right. On Wednesdays, what time does Gerry open the safe for the cash transfer?"

"Fuck if I know."

"Well, I do know," Johnny says. "He opens it at about eleven forty-five. The guys in the armored truck don't show up until about midnight or quarter after. The Weasel goes in there, does a little paperwork drill. Then he sets aside the outgoing cash. Two or three bags. Smaller than a little grocery bag."

"A grocery bag with a couple hundred thousand in it," Goat says.

"Damn right. Then, he sits in there--with the door open--and waits for the transport to show up. I know what he is thinking. The building is shut. The door alarms are on. So he figures if anyone enters the store, he can just shut the vault and reset the time delay."

"But we're already in the store," Goat says, nodding his head with a smile on his face.

"That's right. And we'll have plenty of time to do what we need to do before the transport arrives. Like I said, they don't show up until midnight," Johnny adds. "And we'll be gone by then."

Goat almost immediately objects to the entire plan. "But Gerry will know we did it. So what good does any of this even do?"

"That only matters if we stay here in this shithole. But we're not. We're gonna be long gone. Mexico. Costa Rica. Fuck, I don't know, anywhere but here."

"So we are going to be on the run?" Goat asks.

"Brother, we are going on an adventure," Johnny responds with a smile on his face.

"What about the laundromat?" Goat asks.

"The forty g's?"

"Yeah. Isn't that the whole point?"

"Yep. And we'll get that handled. Our first stop will be a meeting with Mr. Vossen somewhere. We'll give him the money. Arty will be all set."

"But the cops will be all over Arty."

"Of course they will. But not Mr. Vossen. He'll be off back to Holland--"

"What if he rats us out?"

"He won't. He wants the money and he wants to take care of Arty. He won't say anything."

Goat nods. The plan is actually making sense.

"And if we do get busted, we act like the forty K was never there."

"What do you mean 'act like it was never there'? That shit would never fly."

"Not literally, dipshit. I mean we set things up so that no one will know what happened to the money. You know, like drive the car into a river or set it on fire or some shit like that. Tell the cops the money was inside. That money gets written off. So even though we get caught, Mr. Vossen will have his forty large and Arty will have the laundromat."

"Okay. So what about that whole 'we get caught' part. We end up doing time."

Johnny nods his head in agreement and says, "Yeah, but you know what--we're doing time anyway. This isn't a life. This is a prison. Would you really miss this bullshit? Maxi-Mart. The Weasel? Come on."

"You're right. Fuck this bullshit," Goat agrees.

"That's what I'm sayin'."

12

Life is not fair.
Fair didn't make Arty's life the way it is.
I guess I need to make it fair.
Is there something wrong with me wanting to do that?
Or is there something right with me?
Should I accept fate?
Or fight it?
Been accepting it for a long, long time.
And I don't think I like it anymore.

Back at BB's Bar.
Hair metal on the jukebox.
Friday-night crowd.
Smoke.
Depression.
Anger.
Hopelessness.

All masked in music and booze.

Friday night.

Johnny and Goat are talking. Planning.

Now they have something to talk about.

Now they have something to plan.

"We need more time," Goat says.

"More time for what," Johnny asks, "getting the money together?"

"No. We have plenty of time for that. We need more time to get the fuck out of this place. We aren't going to make it far enough," Goat responds, his concern obvious.

"Yeah we will," Johnny says confidently.

"No we won't. The armored truck shows up at midnight. That's like fifteen minutes. When they show up, they're gonna see some shit is wrong. Gerry will tell them everything. The cops will be looking for us. We won't make it to the border."

"Yeah we will," Johnny responds again.

"Fifteen minutes won't even get us close. The Weasel knows our cars . . . he can describe us to a tee . . . he's got pictures of us, for Christ's sake!"

Johnny stares at Goat.

He shakes his head.

Then he says in a low tone, "The Weasel won't be talking to anyone."

Goat is taken aback a bit by this statement. He has a look of slight shock on his face. He responds in a quiet but firm voice. "Bro. Look. I don't like that motherfucker at all . . . but I'm not killing him."

Johnny chuckles. He realizes Goat has the wrong idea. He straightens that out, saying, "Relax. We're not killing him, jackass. Listen--I have this shit covered. Once we get the money, we tie up Gerry, put him in the safe, lock it, turn off all the lights to the store, and we leave a note for the armored drivers."

"A note?"

"Yeah. A note. We tell them that the store had to close early. No one could work. The pickup needed to be postponed. You know, some shit like that."

"You think they'll buy that shit?"

"Even if they don't, it doesn't matter. They'll have to call the cops; once the cops show up, they will see that everything is quiet, or, you know, normal looking. They'll have to call the GM to come down and then . . . then they have to get into the safe."

"But the safe is . . ."

"Time delayed. That's right, motherfucker. No one is getting in until seven o'clock the next morning."

"But by then we'll be . . ."

"Long gone. Probably cracking open some cervezas somewhere down south."

Goat nods his head and cracks a smile. "Damn. That actually sounds pretty fucking good. You make a better criminal than a fucking stock boy."

Johnny smiles back. "Well, let's hope you make a better criminal than a stock boy too. Because you suck as a stock boy."

Goat laughs. Then he gets a serious look on his face and says, "Amen."

13

Who is doing this?
  Who put me here?
  Am I making a bad decision?
  Have I ever made a good one?
  Is this just another bad call in a life
  filled with them?
  I know who put me here.
  And I hate him for it.
    I see him every day.
          In the mirror.
                Staring back at me.

Johnny walks into De Wasserette Laundromat.

"Hey, Johnny!" Arty says with a smile on his face.

Smiling is easy for him. He does not know what is brewing.

"What's going on, Cleaner?"

Arty pauses to think. "I had to change out the thermostat in one of the dryers. It was stuck at around seventy-five degrees. That's

fine for delicates, but not much good for anything else. Too cold. There's nothing worse
than a cold dryer."

"Nothing?" Johnny asks.

Arty pauses to think again. Then: "Nothing.
I mean, if a washer isn't running hot, it's not
because of the washing machine. It's because
of the hot water heater. The washing machine
is still doing what it is supposed to do. So
you can't blame the washing machine. It doesn't
make hot water. But a dryer is different. It is
supposed to make hot air. So if it doesn't
get hot, it has no purpose. What good is it?
And it will still take a person's quarters.
Twenty-five cents for fourteen minutes. But
if they have a pair of jeans in there or an
eighteen-ounce knit sweatshirt, and the tem-
perature only goes up to seventy-five degrees,
they'll be there all night. Things should do
what they are supposed to do. Otherwise, what
is the point?"

Johnny nods his head.

This kid is smarter than he looks.

"How about you, Arty? Do you know what you
are supposed to do?"

Johnny knows the answer.

Arty considers the question for a moment.
He knows the answer, so he gives it: "Yes. Yes

I do. I'm supposed to do laundry. I'm a laundry
guy. That's what I am supposed to do. And here
I am. I come in. I clean lint. I fluff and
fold. I empty quarters. I change thermostats.
That is what I am supposed to do. And I do it."
    Johnny nods his head again. Arty is right.

      He couldn't be any more right.

Johnny knows the answer to another question.
But he asks it anyway too: "What about me,
Arty? What am I supposed to do?"
    Arty tilts his head for a moment. He's
never really thought about this before. Which
is strange. He has thought about most things
before. He speaks as he tries to figure it
out: "Well . . . you work at Maxi-Mart . . .
but . . ."
    "But what?" Johnny asks.
    Arty looks down at the ground, thinking,
then back up again at Johnny.
    Finally, he answers: "Well. I'm not sure that
is what you are supposed to do. I mean, it's
not bad or anything like that . . . but . . .
well . . . I'm here because I'm . . . you
know. I'm different than other people--"
    "Don't worry about other people, Arty,"
Johnny cuts him off.

"I don't worry about other people," Arty replies quickly, "but I do know that I am different. I always have been. And that's fine. But most people--they don't really like me a lot."

"Not true, Arty. Not true," Johnny protests.

"It is true, Johnny. It is true. And that's okay. I'm fine. I'm here. I do what I am supposed to do. But you. You, Johnny. You're smart and you're funny and you're handsome and girls always like you. And, well, I'm not sure if you are supposed to work at Maxi-Mart all your life."

"So, what am I supposed to be doing?" Johnny asks.

"I don't know, Johnny. I don't know. I mean, if you like it, it seems--"

"I don't like it, Arty," Johnny interrupts. "I don't like it at all."

"Then maybe you will do something else one day. Something you like. Something you are good at," Arty suggests.

"Maybe. But I'm not sure what I am good at."

"I know something you're good at," Arty offers.

"What?"

"Taking care of me."

"I don't take care of you, Arty. You are just--"

"It's okay, Johnny. I know you do. You have always taken care of me. Even when we were little. You helped me make food. When I got picked on, you were always there. You stood up for me. You got me this job, here, at the Vossens'. You always take care of me. Maybe that is what you are supposed to do."

"That stuff was a long time ago, Arty. You were younger then. Everybody has a hard time growing up. Besides, you're my brother and you do a lot for me too."

"Yeah, but anybody can do laundry. That's the only thing I do for you."

"But nobody can do it as good as you can, Arty. Nobody."

A washing machine downshifts and goes into its Final Spin cycle.

The conversation shifts with it.

"Where's Mr. Vossen?" Johnny asks.

"He's in the back office."

"I've got to talk to him," Johnny says as he walks toward the rear of the laundromat.

Johnny steps into Mr. Vossen's office.

"Mr. Vossen," Johnny says.

Mr. Vossen looks up from his desk. "Ah.

Johnny. How you been? Did you tell your brother yet?"

Johnny shakes his head. "Nope. I'm not telling him."

"Oh no, Johnny," Mr. Vossen replies, disappointed. "You have to tell him. It's better coming from you than from me."

"No, Mr. Vossen. I'm not telling him, and neither are you."

"Oh no, Johnny. We've got to tell him."

"No, Mr. Vossen. We don't have to tell him."

"Why not?"

"Because I am going to get you the money."

"What?" Mr. Vossen asks, surprised.

"I said *I* am going to get you the money."

Mr. Vossen looks touched. But the look fades quickly. "Johnny--this is--there's no way. How are you going to get forty thousand dollars?"

"Don't worry about that part, Mr. Vossen. But I am going to get it."

Mr. Vossen sits quietly for a moment. He understands that whatever it is Johnny is thinking about doing to get the money, it must be illegal. "Oh no, Johnny. You must not do anything like that for this money. You will get in trouble. You will go to jail."

"I'm not going to jail, Mr. Vossen. And even if I did, I'd rather be there than have Arty lose this place."

"No, Johnny," Mr. Vossen says in a deeply earnest tone. "You do not understand. This will ruin your life." But Johnny pushes back. Hard.

"No, Mr. Vossen. You don't understand. I'm twenty-three years old. I work as a stock boy. I live in an apartment with my drunk mother and my brother. I barely finished high school. I've screwed up everything. *This is it*. I have no life to ruin."

"But you are a very smart person, Johnny," Mr. Vossen retorts.

"I don't think so," Johnny replies. "If I was so smart I wouldn't be here."

"You're still young. You have time. You still have the chance to make something of yourself."

"No, Mr. Vossen, I don't. Even if I busted my ass for the next ten years, what would that get me? Maybe--just maybe--I'd get promoted to night manager at Maxi-Mart."

"See, Johnny! Night manager. Happy times. That's good!"

"No, Mr. Vossen. That's not good. That's not a life. Not for me. Happiness is never going to happen for me. I'm too far gone. But this isn't about me. This is about Arty. He's the one that can be happy. As long as he's here, he will be happy. But if he doesn't have this place . . . well, he'll be worse off than me."

Mr. Vossen listens. He doesn't fully agree with what Johnny is saying, but he understands Johnny's perspective.

"Yes, Johnny. Arty will be happy if you get him this place. But what about you? What if you go to jail?"

"Well," Johnny says with a smile, "I'd still have free laundry in jail."

Mr. Vossen is not amused. "But you will not be free, Johnny. You will not be free."

"There's not much freedom in stocking shelves, Mr. Vossen," Johnny quips.

Mr. Vossen seems out of arguments. "I don't know, Johnny. You need to think about what you are doing."

"I don't need to think. I'm done thinking. You need to think, Mr. Vossen. Will you give Arty the laundromat if I get you the money?"

Mr. Vossen thinks quietly. Finally, he responds. "If you think it will make your brother happy, I will do it. But I don't want to get in trouble. You just get me the money and I will take care of the rest. I will take

care of Arty. He is a good boy. He is a special boy. He will be happy. But you, Johnny.
I worry about you. You could end up in a very
bad place."

"I already am in a very bad place."

"It's not so bad . . ."

"It is bad, Mr. Vossen. It is bad. Anyway,
this isn't about me. It's about Arty. And I
appreciate this, Mr. Vossen. I'll come back in
a few days and tell you how it is all going
to work."

"Okay, Johnny. Okay. I'll see you later."

"Yeah, see you later, Mr. Vossen."

Johnny walks out of the office to the front
of the store.

Arty sees him.

"Did you find Mr. Vossen?"

"Yeah, Arty, I found him."

"You going home now, Johnny?"

"Nope. I'm heading down to BB's to get some
food. You need anything to eat? I can bring
you something back."

"That's okay, Johnny. I had some lunch with
the Vossens. We had *zalmtaart*."

"You had what?"

"*Zalmtaart*. It's Dutch. It's like a pie with
eggs and salmon in it."

"Salmon pie? Does that shit taste good?"

"It is good. Almost as good as KFC."

"Well, that must be pretty good then."

"Yes. It's pretty good. I can get some for you if you want." Arty starts to move toward the refrigerator in the back of the laundromat. "There are some leftovers in the fridge--"

"That's okay, Arty. I'm fine. I'm going to go to BB's. I'll see you later, bud."

"See you later, Johnny."

Johnny walks out the door.

14

What am I supposed to do?
  There are questions in that question.
  What am I supposed to do with my life?
  *What am I supposed to do now that my life
is my life?*
  Now that my life is what it is.
  This isn't what I'm supposed to do.
  I was supposed to do more.
  But I didn't.
  I didn't do anything.
  Nothing.
  That's me.
  Now.
  What am I supposed to do?

BB's Bar.
  Frozen in time.
  "Salmon pie?" Goat asks, somewhat disgusted.
  "Yep. Fuckin' salmon and egg pie."
  "I bet those motherfuckers eat all kinds
of weird shit."

"Salmon and eggs aren't weird. A lot of people eat salmon and eggs," Johnny defends.

"In a pie? What the fuck are you talking about, a lot of people? There are not a lot of people that eat salmon and eggs in a pie."

"Yeah, there are."

"What? Who? Name one person that eats salmon and egg pies. Besides the Vossens," Goat presses.

Johnny thinks for a few seconds, then finds the perfect answer: "My brother," he says proudly.

"Yeah, well, your brother's a little strange," Goat charges, laughing as he responds.

"You're a little fucking strange too" Johnny says.

"Hey man," Goat responds, softening up a bit, "all I'm saying is that there aren't a lot of people in the world that eat salmon pie. That shit is weird."

"Not any weirder than eating fuckin' pickled eggs or fuckin' Vienna sausages or fuckin' Cheez Whiz," Johnny says. "Anyway. Listen. Mr. Vossen is down with the plan."

"Seriously?"

"Yeah. Fully. He's down. He's a little nervous and gave me some fatherly bullshit about getting caught. But he knows it is a logical way out. He gets the money. Arty gets to work at the laundromat. We get the fuck out of this shithole."

"Well. Good," Goat says. He sits for a moment, satisfied with the scenario. Then he thinks through it. "Wait a second. How are we going to work it?"

"Work what?" Johnny responds.

"Getting him the money. The forty g's."

"Man, that's the easy part . . ." Johnny sees Goat's eyes shift focus toward the door. He looks over as well.

There she is.

Jessica.

She makes her way over to Johnny and Goat.

"What's up, sweetheart?" Johnny asks.

"Sweet as diesel fumes," Goat adds playfully.

"Fuck you," Jessica responds not so playfully.

"Lucy," Johnny calls out to the bartender, "SoCo and Coke for the lady!"

Jessica sits down. "And thank you," she says, her eyes moving from Goat to Johnny.

"My pleasure," Johnny says. "You're here early."

"Carla's got some guy at the apartment. A real fucking douchebag. He thinks he owns the place."

Goat tilts his head. "How come I never get Carla?"

"I didn't know you liked girls," Jessica snaps. Johnny laughs.

"Come on," Goat responds. "Seriously. I would treat that girl good."

"I'm sure you would, Goat." Jessica takes on a serious tone: "But I've got bad news for you: You're ugly."

"Ugly as sin," Johnny adds.

"That's fucked up!" Goat says.

"Sorry, brother. She's got a point."

"Sorry, Goat. You asked," Jessica says, smiling.

"How 'bout next time you just lie to me?" Goat says, looking dejected.

"I'm just fucking with you," Jessica says sympathetically.

"I'm not," Johnny says. "You're ugly."

"Up yours," Goat says back at Johnny, then shifts to a happier subject. "Who needs a shot?"

"Let's do it," Johnny says.

"In," says Jessica.

"Lucy," Goat yells, "three shots of Jack."

"Three shots of Jack, comin'," the bartender responds.

"Thanks, big spender," Jessica says, impressed.

"I didn't say I was paying for them," Goat responds.

"You cheap bastard."

"I'm just fucking with you," Goat says, smiling.

Shots are done.

Drinks consumed.

Problems fade.

But they don't go away.

15

They don't go away.
  When I wake up in the morning, I'll still
be: here.
  Not here. But here.
  All the booze won't make them go away.
  I need to do what I am supposed to do.
  What I still can do.

Johnny and Jessica end up at her apartment.
  In her room.
    Small.
      Dark.
        Bed.
          Desk.
            Mirror.
              Brushes.
                Makeup.

Waitress apron hanging on the back of the
chair.

                Dirty.

Wrinkled dollar bills on the desk. Tips.
They've been straightened. Counted.

$64.
Eight-hour shift.

In bed.

Jessica is smoking a cigarette. Johnny is
staring at the ceiling.

"What's up with you?" she asks.

"What do you mean?"

"I mean what's up with you? You're all quiet
and shit. What's going on?"

"I'm just thinking."

"Yeah. No shit. What are you thinking about?"

"This."

"This?" Jessica says, slightly annoyed.
"This what?"

"This. Us."

"What about us?"

"Us. Our lives. Our existence. Do you think
this is it?" Johnny asks genuinely.

Jessica is pragmatic. "Yeah. Of course this
is it. This is how life goes. You're born. You
go to school. You get a job. Then you work. You
meet some people along the way. You get old
and die. That's it. What did you expect? Fame
and fortune?"

She says "fame and fortune" with a hint of disgust--as if it is a childish fantasy.

Johnny picks up on that. He's a little embarrassed. "No. Not fame and fortune. But something. Something bigger."

"Bigger than what?" Jessica asks.

"Bigger than Maxi-Mart. Bigger than BB's Bar. Bigger than this. You know, like the rest of the world. Don't you want to see it?"

Jessica thinks about that for a moment, but not for too long. She already knew her answer, and once she checked her thoughts, she gives it. "I don't know. I think it's pretty much all the same."

Johnny lets that sink in. Then he says: "I don't."

Jessica tries to de-escalate the conversation. "Well, the grass is always greener on the other side."

The de-escalation doesn't work. "Well, I don't want to take someone else's word about that."

Jessica is silent for a moment. She understands what he is saying--or trying to say. She tries to find an out for him--and for herself. "It doesn't matter. You can't just leave here. Neither can I. That's not the way the world works. So we might as well make the best of it."

"Make the best of it? Make the best of this?" Johnny asks earnestly. "I'm not going to. I can't. I can't convince myself that this is it. This shit is supposed to be my fucking destiny? I was put on this earth to be a fucking stock boy at a fucking Maxi-Mart?" Jessica is silent. Johnny continues: "No. I cannot convince myself of that. There has to be more. There has to be."

"Am I supposed to feel bad because I'm a waitress? I've got to make a fucking living. I've got to pay rent."

"Yeah, but like this? Those people you wait on every day--they've got money. Houses. Cars. Why? Because they were born into the right families? Because someone picked up the tab for them to go to college? They aren't any smarter than you. They sure as shit aren't any harder working. They just got lucky."

"Really? Really? None of this is on you? Or me? I fucked up a lot of things. No one made me cut classes in high school. No one made me quit community college. I did that. You can't put your shit on someone else. This is where I am right now. I put myself here. You put yourself where you are. We can't blame the rest of the world. If you don't like where you are, fix it."

"I'm gonna try."

The saxophone intro to Bob Seger's song "Turn the Page" suddenly blasts from outside the bedroom. "What the fuck is that?" Johnny asks.

"I told you. The guy thinks he owns the place."

"But whose fucking Bob Seger is that?"

"It's his. He brought over a bunch of his own CDs. Nothing but the best. Bob Seger. Boston. The Eagles."

"Great."

"At least you don't have to live here," Jessica says.

"Neither do you," Johnny tells Jessica.

She looks at him.

She sees something there.

Some thought.

Some idea.

But she doesn't know what it is.

She can't quite figure it out.

16

You don't have to live here, she said.
  She's right.
  I don't.
  I'm the thing that is keeping me here.
    Me.
  Tonight is the night.

Johnny and Goat stand in front of the giant Maxi-Mart freezers.

"You need to get to the chicken patties," Gerry tells them. "Put them in F7. That will make enough room for the egg and bacon breakfast burritos in F4. Got that?"

"Yeah, I got it," Johnny replies unenthusiastically.

"What about you, *George*," Gerry says to Goat.

"Don't call me George."

"Do you got it?" Gerry pushes.

"Yeah. I got it," Goat answers.

"Good. Then get to it, *boys*," Gerry says sneeringly.

Goat has had enough. He needs to check this

attitude from Gerry. "Who the fuck are you calling boys?"

"Sorry, *George,*" Gerry replies, now obviously and intentionally digging at Goat.

"I said don't call me George, *Weasel.*"

"You better not push it," Gerry says, raising his finger, pointing at Goat. Then he lowers his finger, turns, and walks away.

"Chill out, man. Just relax," Johnny tells Goat.

"Fuck that guy," Goat replies angrily.

"Just fucking calm down. You're going to fuck up this whole plan if you act like this."

"I'm not going to fuck this up. But I'm also not going to get treated like a punk."

"Just don't worry about that shit right now. We have a mission. Stay focused on it," Johnny pleads.

Goat stares at the ground. He takes a breath. "All right. Fine."

"Fine. Good," Johnny says. "Now let's go take care of those fuckin' chicken patties. We got at least three more pallets."

The two walk through the cavernous warehouse store toward the back, through a curtain of plastic slats, and into a massive refrigerated receiving area.

As they walk, they think through the plan.

Johnny wonders if they have thought through everything.

Goat is not even nervous. His sole focus is on Gerry, and the opportunity to humiliate him.

There is a pallet filled with chicken.
Chicken patties.
Breaded chicken patties.
Frozen breaded chicken patties.

Johnny wheels a pallet jack into position, then moves the handle up and down, elevating the pallet a few inches into the air. He begins to pull back the pallet as Goat steadies the chicken boxes with his hand.

They wheel the pallet out into the store and make their way to freezer F7.

They begin stocking the freezer with chicken patties.

Johnny says quietly, "So, you good?"

"Yeah, man. I'm good."

"You know the plan?"

"I know the plan, man. I know the plan. We've gone over it a thousand times. I got it."

"Any last questions?" Johnny asks.

"Yeah. I got a question. How many *chiquitas* can I get in Mexico with a hundred grand?"

Johnny smiles. "Plenty."

They slowly place the last of the frozen chicken patties in the freezer and shut the door.

"You ready?" Johnny asks.

"I sure am," Goat replies.

Johnny takes a deep breath.

"Let's fucking do it."

They return the pallet to the refrigerated receiving area.

Johnny checks his watch. 11:37.

"Get the gear," he tells Goat.

"On it." Goat walks behind one of the large shelving units and picks up a box they'd hidden beneath some cleaning rags.

Inside the box is:

Ritz crackers.
Jalapeño Cheez Whiz.
Hostess cherry pies.
Beef jerky.
A bag of disposable lighters.
Two bottles of Jack Daniel's.
A coil of nylon rope.
Four rolls of duct tape.
And two big duffel bags.

They take the box and walk out of the receiving area, into the main floor of the store, then to a position where they can see the vault. Gerry is standing in front of the walk-in vault reading a piece of paper.

Johnny and Goat watch him. Finally, he checks his watch, approaches a small wall safe, and opens it. From there he retrieves a key. He uses the key to open a small security box on the wall, where he types a code into a keypad to open the vault.

There are three loud beeps, then one long one as the locking devices of the vault door move into the open position. Gerry moves one final lever, and the vault is open.

He walks inside.

Johnny and Goat look at each other.

This is the point of no return.

After this, everything will be different.

On the run?

Mexico?

South America?

Prison?

This is the moment of decision.

Go or no-go.

Johnny breaks the silence: "Once you're in position, I'll go in."

That settles it. No more discussion. No more thinking.

It's go time.

"Got it," Goat says.

Goat leans down to the supply box and gets out the rope and the duct tape. He quietly steps from behind the shelves and moves toward the vault, staying hidden from view by keeping a partition between him and the vault. Once in position, he looks at Johnny and nods.

Johnny nods back. He begins to move.

He approaches the vault.

His mind is racing at first but then, in an instant, it settles.

He is focused now.

Johnny reaches a point where he can see Goat hidden outside the vault and Gerry working inside. He nods at Goat with a look that says, *here we go.* Goat nods back. Johnny shifts his eyes to Gerry.

"Hey, Gerry," he calls.

Gerry, concentrating on his paperwork, is annoyed. "What?"

"There's no egg and bacon breakfast burritos out back."

"What? Yeah there are," Gerry responds. Johnny can see Gerry is irritated he has to deal with these petty problems.

"No, there aren't. I just came from back there."

"Yes, there are. They are in area nine of receiving. The back corner."

Johnny approaches the door of the vault.

He can sense it now. He forces himself to stay calm.

"We looked there," Johnny says.

"Well, look again."

"I'm telling you," Johnny says, "they are not there."

Gerry is quiet. The look on his face says that it is hard for him to believe that people can be so stupid, so incompetent.

"Goddamnit. You guys are worthless. You can't do anything on your own." Gerry stands up and looks hard at Johnny, almost pitiful, then says, "Let's go then. I'll show you."

Johnny turns and begins to walk away from the vault.

Gerry follows him.

In his peripheral vision, Johnny picks up Goat in his hiding place. But Johnny continues to look straight ahead.

Gerry walks past Goat, not seeing him.

As soon as Gerry is past, Goat steps out behind Gerry and puts him in a choke hold.

Gerry has no idea what is happening. He is confused, then horrified.

Johnny hears this unfold and turns around.

Gerry's and Johnny's eyes lock.

Gerry is comforted almost instantly when he makes eye contact with Johnny.

Johnny sees the relief in Gerry's eyes.

He thinks I am going to help him.

Johnny gets close enough to Gerry and gut punches him.

Gerry keels over.

Goat trips up Gerry's legs and they collapse to the ground.

The choke hold is having its intended effect:

Gerry goes unconscious.

17

There's no turning back now.

"He's out, man, I think he's out!" Goat shouts.

"He's out. He's out," Johnny replies. "I'll get his hands."

Johnny grabs a roll of duct tape.

He makes quick work of Gerry's hands, taping them up, secure.

Goat lets up on the choke hold, and they drag him into the vault.

In a moment, Gerry wakes up.

"Don't kill me. Please. Don't kill me."

"SHUT THE FUCK UP, WEASEL!" Goat yells.

"Get the bags," Johnny says in a firm but calm voice.

Goat walks out of the vault.

"Don't kill me," Gerry pleads.

"We're not going to kill you," Johnny responds, "as long as you shut the fuck up."

Johnny studies the inside of the vault.

This was one of the unknowns.

One of the only things he couldn't plan in detail.

He sees a phone mounted on the wall.

He rips it off.

He sees a keypad on the wall inside the vault.

He smashes it with the handset of the phone.

Gerry flinches with each strike.

Johnny slides the destroyed phone out of the vault on the floor.

He looks at his watch.

11:47.

Johnny grabs Gerry's key chain, rips it from his belt loop, and puts the keys in his pocket.

Then he drags Gerry to the corner of the vault and begins to tie him more securely with the rope. He ties and tapes his feet together.

Goat reenters with the box, sets it down, and gets out the duffel bags. "How much is here, Weasel?" he barks.

"How much what?" Gerry responds meekly.

"How much money, dipshit?"

"Money?" Gerry asks, still not understanding what is happening.

"Yeah," Goat says. "How much money is in here?"

"Oh. About two hundred and eighty thousand."

"Bingo," Goat says with a smile.

"Wait," Gerry says as he begins to put the scene together, "you guys are robbing this place?"

"Shut the fuck up," Johnny tells him.

With that, Johnny and Goat begin to load money from the shelves into the duffel bags.

"I pulled the phone out of there," Johnny says, nodding to the wall, "and smashed a keypad over there."

"Looks good," Goat approves.

They work quickly loading the bags.

Goat places in the last stack of money.

"All right, that's it. Let's go." Goat slings one duffel of money over his shoulder and bends down next to the box. "Here," Goat says as he picks up a can of Cheez Whiz and throws it at Gerry, "have some Cheez Whiz."

Johnny walks over to Gerry and kneels down. "All right, Gerry. What combo do I put in to lock the door?"

"Don't lock me in here!" Gerry shouts.

"I'm either going to lock you in here or I'm cutting out your fucking tongue. The choice is yours."

"Gerry."

"What?"

"Gerry. G-E-R-R-Y. That's the combo."

"Gerry? You mean your name? You made the combo your name?" Johnny says.

"Yeah. Gerry," Gerry replies, dejected.

"What a fucking nerd," Goat adds.

"Let's go," Johnny says.

They move toward the door of the vault.

They step outside and stare at Gerry as they swing the door shut.

Johnny punches the code into the keypad.

G.
  E.
   R.
    R.
     Y.

The panel makes one long beep as the vault's locking mechanisms move into place.

Three more short beeps signal it is locked.

They clean up the area, shut the wall safe, and walk toward the front door.

Johnny opens the door with a key from Gerry's key chain, conveniently marked:

"Maxi-Mart Front Door."

"Give me the note," Johnny says.

Goat reaches into the box, pulls out a note, and hands it to Johnny.

Johnny sticks the note on the door with a piece of duct tape.

The note reads:

Union Bank Armored Car Crew,

I apologize, but several employees, including myself, were severely sick. There were not enough replacement workers for the shift, so we canceled it. I will contact your headquarters to reschedule a cash transfer either tomorrow afternoon or evening.

Sorry for the inconvenience.

Gerry Lunstrum
Night Manager
Maxi-Mart

"Think they'll buy it?" Goat asks.

"They might. But it doesn't matter," Johnny replies as he checks his watch.

11:54. "Let's go."

They carry their loot through the store, toward the back.

Johnny stops at the electrical panel and turns off the lights.

It goes dark.

They close the garage door of the loading dock.

Walk out of the door beside it.

Johnny takes out the keys and locks the door.

They walk toward Johnny's car.

A 1982 Buick Century wagon.

Johnny puts the keys in the ignition, fires it up, and puts the car in reverse.

As he turns to back out of the spot, Goat speaks. "That was easy."

"We're not done yet," Johnny says as he puts the car in drive and starts out of the parking lot.

"I know," Goat chuckles, "but you got to admit that shit was easy."

"Yeah. It was. You should have seen the look on Weasel's face."

"When I grabbed him?"

"Yeah. That was good. But when I hit him? He was scared shitless."

"Good. That fucking weasel."

In the distance, headlights approach.

"Here is the Union truck," Johnny says as he checks his watch. "Twelve oh-two."

"You're a little late, motherfuckers!" Goat says, laughing.

The two vehicles pass each other.

"Do you think they're gonna call the cops or anything?" Goat asks.

"They might. But they probably won't. They've got a bunch of other pickups to manage on their route. They're just another couple of working stiffs like us. They'll see that sign and leave--they want to get home to momma."

"I hope so," Goat says, finally revealing a little nervousness.

"Even if they call the cops, we've got plenty of time. The cops will call dispatch. They'll have to track down the number for the owner of the store. The owner will call the store. Then he'll call Gerry's house. Then he'll get out of bed and drive down and then they will still have to open the safe. And the time delay doesn't turn off until seven A.M. We're good. Trust me, man, we're good."

Goat nods. "Right on."

"Next stop, Dell's Diner."

"Dell's Diner?"

"Yep. That's where we're meeting Mr. Vossen."

18

The Union Bank armored truck pulls up in front of Maxi-Mart.

Its brakes squeal quietly as it comes to a stop.

The driver gets out on one side. The guard gets out on the other.

The driver notices the darkness. And then the note.

Puzzled.

"What the hell is that?" the guard says as they walk toward the door.

"It's a note."

"What's it say?"

The driver stands and reads the note: "Says everybody's sick. Call to reschedule."

"That settles that," the guard says. "Let's go."

"We gotta call it in," the driver replies.

"What?"

"We gotta call it in. That's the procedure."

The guard presses his face against the glass and shields the light from the parking

94

lot lamps with his hands so he can see inside. "The place is closed. No one's in there. Everything looks normal."

"Yeah, well, we still need to call it in. It's the procedure."

"Fine."

They get back in the truck.

The driver lifts a radio mic to his face and presses the push-to-talk button.

19

It's come to this.
  I did it.
  I'm not done yet.
  But I did it.
  I'm scared, nervous, paranoid.
  Hunted.
  Haunted.
  Horrified.

And free.

        The Buick.
            Decelerates.
                Off-ramp.
                    Right at the light.
                        There it is.
        "Dell's Diner."
Pull in.
Stop.
Wait.
"Where the fuck is he?" Goat asks.

"Probably on his way," Johnny responds. He checks his watch. "We're early."

"Well, he better get here soon."

"He will."

Johnny gets out of the car and opens the rear hatch. He pulls out one of the duffel bags, carries it to the front of the car, and gets back in.

"Gonna count it?" Goat asks.

"Not now. There's plenty. I'm just getting Mr. Vossen his money."

Johnny opens the bag and then cracks his door, so the interior light comes on.

"Cash," Goat says.

"Damn right."

Money.
All denominations.
Lots of it.

Johnny begins to count. He hands his first bundle to Goat.

"That's ten. Put it in that bag," Johnny says, motioning to a plastic bag on the floor at Goat's feet.

Goat places the money in the bag. Johnny keeps counting.

"Twenty," Johnny says as he hands Goat the next pile.

"Twenty g's for Mr. Vossen," Goat says with a smile.

Thirty.

Forty.

Johnny keeps counting.

"I thought we were only giving him forty?" Goat asks.

"I'm throwing another thirty in there."

"Another thirty?"

"Ten for Mr. Vossen. Twenty for Arty."

"What the fuck is Arty gonna do with twenty grand? Buy Perfecto fucking laundry detergent? He won't know what to do with that kind of money."

"I'm not giving it to him. It's for him. I'm giving it to Mr. Vossen. Mr. Vossen will take care of him. If Arty ever needs anything, Mr. Vossen is good people."

"You must really trust the old man."

"Yeah. I do."

"You really think Arty can run the laundromat by himself? Like, the business side of stuff. Bills and taxes and all that."

"Mr. Vossen is going to help him before he leaves for Holland. Set him up with his accountant. It's a friend of his. He will run the books. Pay the bills. All that stuff. Arty will run the place."

"For free?"

"Nah. Mr. Vossen's friend will take a little cut. A small salary. Nothing big. But it's worth it. Arty needs him. Mr. Vossen will track it all from Holland. Review the numbers and stuff. He will take a little cut too--but he really just wants to take care of Arty."

"He's a good man."

"Indeed."

20

Police cruiser pulls into the Maxi-Mart parking lot.

Police officer gets out of the squad car.

The driver and the guard get out of the armored car.

"You the boys that called this in?" the officer asks.

"Well, we called our dispatch. They called you."

"But you two were first on the scene?"

"Yep."

"And they said you found a note?"

"That we did." The driver reaches into his pocket and pulls out the note.

The officer reads the note, then asks, "Did you guys find anything else? Notice anything else?"

"Place looks closed. Nobody inside. No lights or anything. Just procedure to call it in."

The police officer walks up to the window, presses his face against it, and looks inside the store. "Yeah," he says, "looks normal. But I gotta call it in. Protocol."

"The place is just closed," the guard says.

"Yeah. But I gotta call it in." He grabs his lapel mic and keys the push-to-talk. "Delta Tango, this is Mike-Four out on the 298, west end on 10-59. Do you have the emergency contact for this place?"

"Stand by," the voice on the radio responds. "Is that the Maxi-Mart?"

"10-4."

"We've got a number for the general manager and one for the alarm security company."

"There was no alarm here."

"10-4. I can give the general manager a call."

"10-4. I'll be standing by on scene."

The guard and the driver get back in their armored vehicle.

The officer gets back in his cruiser.

They wait.

21

I trust him.
   I better be able to trust him.
   I trust him.
   Where is he?

Car pulls in next to Johnny's.
   1989 Honda Accord hatchback.
   The door opens.
   Mr. Vossen gets out.
   He walks over to Johnny's car, peers in, sees Johnny and Goat, then opens the back door and gets in.
   "How you doin', Mr. Vossen?" Johnny asks.
   "Very nervous."
   "Well, now you can be very nervous and very rich."
   Goat hands the money to Mr. Vossen.
   "Thank you," Mr. Vossen says.
   "There's seventy thousand in there, Mr. Vossen."
   "Seventy? We agreed on forty."

"It's okay. There is an extra twenty for Arty. And an extra ten for you."

"You want me to give the extra twenty thousand to Arty?"

"No. Hell no. You keep it. You hold onto it. When he needs something, tell him to come to you. You help him get what he needs."

"When he needs something like what?"

"I don't know. New clothes. New shoes. Set him up a bank account. Show him how to deposit and withdraw money. You know, that kind of stuff. And the other ten is just for you. To take care of yourself while you take care of Arty."

"Okay, Johnny. I can do that. Like I said, I'll spend some time making sure he knows what to do. My accountant will be helpful too. He knows the business."

"Can you call to check in on him once a week too once you get back to Holland?"

"Yes. Yes, I will. That will keep him happy."

"What makes him happy is the laundromat. Working. Cleaning. You know that. That's what is important. That's what makes him happy."

"Well, then, this will make him happy." Mr. Vossen is quiet for a moment, then says, "You know, you make him happy too Johnny. What should I tell him happened to you?"

"Just tell him I got in some trouble and had to run away."

"When should I tell him you are coming back?"

"Tell him . . . just tell him I'll come back when I can. Tell him it might be a while."

Mr. Vossen listens. He tilts his head.

He knows.

"You are never coming back, are you?"

Johnny knows he knows.

"No, Mr. Vossen. I don't think so."

"And you, Goat? Are you ever coming back?"

"Nope. Not me," Goat replies. "This is it."

Mr. Vossen looks sad for a moment.

Then, he clutches the money and says, "Well, I better go."

Mr. Vossen opens the door and gets out of the car.

He starts to walk away.

He stops.

He comes back.

Johnny rolls down his window.

"You are a good brother, Johnny. A very good brother," Mr. Vossen says.

Mr. Vossen walks back to his car.

He gets in.

He drives away.

The boys sit silently for a minute.

"Well. We going to Dell's?" Goat asks.

Johnny does not respond.

"Are we going to Dell's?" Goat asks again, louder.

"Are you serious?" Johnny responds.

"I'm hungry as shit."

"Well, get yourself some Cheez Whiz, cause we're not stopping until we get south of the border except for gas. Damn."

"All right. Fine. Let's go then."

Ignition.

Rolling.

Highway.

"How long until we hit Mex?" Goat asks.

"About five," Johnny responds.

"What time is it?"

"Twelve forty-eight."

"We'll be there before the morning shift shows up at Maxi-Mart."

22

Parking lot.
   Cadillac.
      Black.
         New.

The general manager of Maxi-Mart gets out of his Cadillac.

Midthirties.
   Fit.
      Slick hair.
         Frustrated.

"Good evening, sir," the police officer says.
"Yeah. Let me see the note."
The officer hands the note over to the manager. He reads it quickly.
"Bullshit. This is bullshit," the manager says.
The manager reaches in his pocket.

FINAL SPIN

    Gets keys.
     Opens front door.

  The police officer motions to the manager,
the guard, and the driver to let him go first.
  He holds a flashlight in his left hand,
places his right hand on his holster, opens
the door, and walks in.
  He looks around.
  Light into darkness.
  Nothing.
  A half a minute passes.
  "All clear," he calls out. "Come on in."
  The manager, guard, and driver walk in.
  The manager walks to the office area out-
side the vault.
  There is a piece of paper on the wall in a
piece of corkboard: EMPLOYEE SCHEDULE.
  The manager reads it out loud. "Wednesday
night. Lunstrum."
  He walks over to a desk, sits down, and
flips open a Rolodex.
  He finds what he is looking for.
  Picks up phone.
    Dials.
  Eventually, he talks.
  "Yes, I'm looking for Mr. Lunstrum. Mr.

Geraldo Lunstrum. Yes. I'm the general manager here at Maxi-Mart. I'm not sure, but I am
trying to figure that out. Yes, ma'am. Okay. I
will. Thank you."

He hangs up.

"Lunstrum, the night manager who was supposed to be working tonight and supposedly
wrote this note, is not at home. His wife said
he is here. Something is wrong."

"The vault looks secure," the officer says.

The manager looks around.

Snoops around.

Across desks. In drawers. He looks in a
garbage can.

He freezes, then reaches in, pulls out a
phone, and holds it out in front of him.

"Broken phone?" the officer asks.

"Yes, a broken phone that came from inside
the fucking vault!" the manager says, with his
statement finishing as a scream.

"Calm down, sir," the officer says before
keying the mic on his radio. "Delta Tango, I
have a possible 10-70 at the west side Maxi-
Mart. Request backup and crime-scene team.
Building not secure at this time."

The manager looks puzzled. "What do you
mean, 'building not secure'?"

"I mean there may be suspects here. In the building."

"Bullshit. They're long gone!"

"Calm down!"

"Calm down? I just got robbed! And we have no idea who did it or where they are. But they aren't in here, I can tell you that!" the manager shouts.

"The alarm never went off."

"And?"

"Let's check inside the vault."

"Even the override takes a half hour to open."

"Well, let's get it started. This kind of thing is usually an inside job. Who else was working tonight?"

The manager settles down as he realizes the police officer might have something to offer. He walks back over to the schedule.

"Jonathon MacDermott and George Martinez. Stock boys."

"You know these guys?" the officer asks.

"Yeah. I mean, I know who they are."

"Do you think they could have done this?"

"I don't know. But I guarantee it wasn't Lunstrum. I can tell you that," the manager says.

"Well, let's give these two a call," the officer says. "You got their numbers?"

The manager walks back to the Rolodex and flips it open.

He picks up the phone.

23

Jessica.
    BB's Bar.
        Nervous.
            Looking around.
            For Johnny.

She takes a seat at the bar.
"How ya doin'?" the barmaid asks.
"You seen Johnny?" Jessica asks.
"Nope. Not tonight. You want anything?"
"Yeah . . . just a . . . just an orange juice."
"You got it, honey," she says, and then announces, "last call!"
Jessica produces a fake smile.

She's scared.

      Scared of something.

          But at the same time: settled.

24

Highway rest stop.
   Cracked concrete.
      Flickering, fluorescent lights.
         Trash, scattered.
   Lonely.
      Four gas pumps.
         Window-cleaning stations.
            Dry.
Sign reads: FRANNIE'S—FOOD. FUEL. FUN.

1989 Chevy Blazer pulls up slowly.
   Good condition.
      Brown with tan trim.
         Light bar.

The sheriff gets out.
   Almost fifty.
      Wire-rimmed glasses.
         Plain, civilian clothes.
            He's not on duty.
               Overweight.
                  Soft.

He wanted to retire a few years ago.
    Life got in the way.
        So he's still in the game.
           But not really.
                He just wants to ride out
                his time . . .

He walks into the store.
    A woman is behind the counter.
        Fortysomething.
           But it has been a hard forty-
           something years.
           Smoker.

"Good evenin', Sheriff," she says.

"How ya doin', Beth?" he asks.

"Better now that you came in. What can I getcha?"

"How 'bout a nice big ole cup o' coffee. And a cinnamon roll."

"You got it," Beth replies with a smile. "What are you doing out so late?"

"Ah, two of my deputies downtown are sick. I've got to go on duty and cover for one of them in a couple of hours. No sense in goin' home."

"Well, make yourself at home here then."

"How 'bout some TV?"

JOCKO WILLINK

"Sure. Ain't much on though."

She turns on the TV.
   Hands over the cup of coffee.
      And the cinnamon roll.

25

Jessica approaches the door.
Hesitates.
Reconsiders:

Maybe just walk away.
Leave it.
Do it alone.

But she can't.
She exhales.
Rings the doorbell.
Noise inside. It's late. Muffled voice. Another muffled voice. Movement.
The door opens.
Arty.

Clean, plaid pajamas.
Pressed.

"Hey, Arty. Is Johnny here?"
Silence. Thought.
"I don't think so."

"Did he have work tonight?"

"I'm not sure."

"Well, is he here or not?"

"I don't think so."

"You don't think so?"

"I don't think so."

More silence.

"Do you think you could check?"

Arty tilts his head as he tries to understand.

He understands.

"Oh yeah. Of course. Sure."

He knows he should say something else.

"Do you want to come in?"

"That would be great."

Arty steps back from the door.

Jessica walks in.

He leads her to a kitchenette.

Vinyl floor. Warped.

Table.

Three chairs.

Arty pulls one out for her.

Jessica sits down. She's not comfortable.
But not uncomfortable.

Arty knows he should say something else.

"Do you want something to drink?"

"No . . . no thank you."

"Okay. Well. I'll go check."

He walks out, and up the stairs.

She crosses her legs, nervously.

Arty returns.

"He's not here."

Jessica looks angry.

She stands up.

But her face twists from anger to sadness in a flash.

The sadness forces her back into the chair.

She starts to cry.

Arty is nervous now.

> He does not know how to handle these things.

"Do you want something to drink? Some tea?"

Jessica senses the pure kindness of Arty. "Okay," she tells him as she tries to control her tears.

Arty puts a kettle on and takes out a box of tea inscribed with Dutch writing.

Jessica watches him.

"Do you mind if I wait here for him? I really need to talk to him."

"Sure," Arty says. After a moment, he adds,

"Maybe I'll have some tea with you, if that's okay."

"That would be nice, Arty. That would be nice."

26

The manager is thumbing through the Rolodex.

He comes to the name George Martinez.

Pulls out the card and hands it to the officer.

The officer picks up the phone.

Dials.

Listens for a moment.

"He's not fucking home," the manager says.

"It's best to be sure," says the officer as he continues to listen.

"Look. We got robbed. I don't know where the night manager is. These two guys are nowhere to be found. It must be them."

"Let's be sure. Nothing is worse than a red herring this early in an investigation." The officer hangs up the phone.

"No one?" asks the manager.

"No one," says the officer.

The manager looks at the officer, disappointed.

"Let's try the other guy."

The manager shakes his head as he walks back over to the Rolodex.

He pulls out the card labeled 'JONATHON MAC-DERMOTT.'

27

The phone rings and startles both Jessica and Arty.

"I'll get that," Arty says.

He picks up the phone.

"Hello. No, he is not. I do not know. Not that I know of. Yes. I'm his brother. Yes. No. You're welcome. Goodbye."

Arty hangs up the phone.

Jessica looks at him. Her look says: *Who was it?*

It takes a few seconds for Arty to register that look.

He answers the look: "It was the police."

"The police?" Jessica says.

"The police."

Jessica looks at him. Her look says: *What did they want?*

Arty registers the look (a little quicker this time) and answers it: "They were looking for Johnny."

"Johnny?"

"Yes. Johnny."

"But you don't know where he is."

"No. I don't. Maybe he is at BB's," Arty suggests.

"He's not at BB's. BB's is closed now. I was just there." She pauses. Then adds, "Can I have some more tea?"

"Sure. It's good. It's from Holland."

"It is good. Thanks, Arty."

Arty gets another bag of Pickwick tea.

He puts it in her mug and pours in water from the kettle.

It steeps.

Darkening the water.

28

The night sky is endless.
   Stars.
   Galaxies.
   Forever.
I am nothing in their presence.
Nothing.
And yet it all revolves around me.
I am the center of my universe.
And all the while: I am nothing.
Nothing. Nowhere.

They continue down the highway.
      Open road.
            Darkness in the distance.
            Glow of the dashboard.

"How we doin' fuel wise?" Goat asks.
   "We're going to have to stop pretty soon."
   "Good, man. I'm fucking starving."
   "Have some more Cheez Whiz."
   "No. No more fucking Cheez Whiz."

"In a couple of days, you'll be eating whatever you want, whenever you want it--provided by a nice Mexican señorita."

"Damn straight."

Silence.

Time.

"How much longer do we have?" Goat asks.

"Just a few more hours."

"Good. We're almost out," Goat says, shaking a near-empty can of Cheez Whiz.

29

The officer hangs up the phone.

"See," the manager barks, "he's not there. I'm telling you. These guys are the thieves. Can't you put out a call for them?"

"I can," responds the officer before keying his radio. "This is Mike-Four."

"Go ahead, Mike-Four," the voice of a dispatcher responds.

"I'm gonna need you to run some names for me. I'm gonna need vehicles registered and we might need to put out an APB on some suspects."

"Standing by."

"First is Martinez, George. Second is Mac-Dermott, Jonathon."

"Is that M-C or M-A-C?"

"Mary, Adam, Charles."

"10-4. Stand by."

The manager grumbles, "Couple of fucking idiots."

Silence.

Then, the dispatcher: "Mike-Four, how copy?"

"This is Mike-Four, go ahead."

"Check. I got a vehicle registered to one Jonathon MacDermott. 1982 Buick Century wagon. Dark blue. Nothing registered for George Martinez."

"10-4. Can you put an APB out on that Buick?"

"On it."

30

The sheriff sips his coffee.
He's in plain clothes.

Pair of jeans.
Flannel shirt.
Utility jacket.

His duty belt is barely noticeable.
Pistol in holster.
Radio on his hip with lapel mic
clipped to the collar of his flannel.

Nothing is on TV.
Volume off.
But he watches it.

The lapel mic of his radio breaks squelch.
He reaches down to his duty belt and
increases the volume.
It's loud now.

An announcement. Beth listens.

"This is an all-points bulletin being issued for a blue 1982 Buick Century wagon. One white male, age twenty-three, dark hair, pale complexion. One Hispanic male, twenty-four, black hair, dark complexion. Suspects involved in a robbery. Should be considered armed and dangerous."

The sheriff turns the radio back down.
Sips coffee.

Outside, a car pulls up.
Beth looks outside.
"I'll be damned."

The sheriff looks outside.
"Son-of-a-bitch."

There it is: a blue 1982 Buick Century wagon.

The sheriff tries to relax.
"Might not be them."

The doors open.

Johnny and Goat get out.

"And it might be," says the sheriff.

"What are we going to do?" the woman asks, panicked.

"Just stay calm, Beth. We are all alone out here. There's no backup for at least a half hour. Just stay calm. Serve 'em what they want. Nice and normal. As soon as they head on down the road, I'll call 'em in."

"Yes, sir," she replies. "Stay calm. Yes, sir."

Goat walks in. "How ya doing?" he asks the woman.

"Just fine, sir," she replies.

"We want to fill it up, please. Pump four."

Goat takes a wad of money out of his pocket. He hands the woman two twenties.

The sheriff watches.

He knows.

The woman takes the two twenties.

"Thank you," she says. A little too calm. But Goat doesn't notice.

"You got a bathroom in here?" Goat asks.

"Yessir. Straight through the back. First door on the right," she says, pointing toward the back of the store.

"Thanks," Goat says.

Goat walks by the sheriff.

They make eye contact.

Goat gives him a nod and a small smile.

The sheriff does the same.

Outside, Johnny has started the gas pumping.

He heads inside.

The woman sees.

"Oh my God," she says.

"Just stay calm," the sheriff replies, obviously nervous.

Johnny walks into the store.

"Evenin'," he says to the woman.

"Hello, sir," she responds.

The sheriff glances over his shoulder at Johnny.

Their eyes meet.

"Sir," Johnny says.

The sheriff nods. "Good evening."

Johnny moves toward the snack section of the store.

Beef jerky.

Cheetos.

Trail mix.

Sunflower seeds.

He picks up various foods.
Considers them.
Puts them back.
Checks others.

Finally decides: Hostess cherry pie. Large can of Pringles potato chips.

He heads back toward the counter, the woman, and the cash register.

"Find what you were looking for?" she asks.

"Sure did. Thanks."

He places the items on the counter.
She picks them up.
Enters the information into the register.

"Three forty-eight," she says.

"Three forty-eight," he replies.

Johnny reaches into his pocket and pulls out a wad of money.

He hands the woman a twenty-dollar bill.

As he does, the sheriff's radio breaks squelch again.

"Victor six-eight, this is dispatch."

The radio startles Johnny.

He looks quickly at the sheriff.
Johnny's quick movement startles the sheriff.

The sheriff reacts.
He stands up and draws his .38 caliber service revolver from his holster.
He aims it at Johnny.

As that is happening, Goat walks out of the bathroom.
He immediately sees the sheriff drawn down on Johnny.
He goes into stealth mode.

He crouches down between the aisles.
He looks for a weapon.
He instantly sees a jar of Skippy peanut butter.

"Don't move," the sheriff is saying to Johnny. "Don't move a goddamn muscle."
The sheriff's voice is tense with fear.

This is not the night he wanted.

Goat maneuvers into position, staying behind the shelves in the aisles.

When he gets close enough, he makes his move.

He quietly steps behind the sheriff, the peanut butter jar raised above his head.

The woman's eyes widen, and she makes a small gasp.

The sheriff reacts to this, and turns around just as Goat begins his downswing with the jar of peanut butter.

Just as the jar hits the sheriff's head, he fires off one round from his pistol.

The jar breaks.
>   The sheriff is knocked unconscious.
>   Goat is hit:
>   Gut-shot.

The woman screams: "Don't kill me!"

"We're not gonna kill you," Johnny yells back.

"I'm shot!" Goat mutters.

"We gotta get outta here!" Johnny tells him.

"You killed the sheriff!" the woman yells.

"That guy is a sheriff?" Goat says, shocked.

"A cop?" Johnny adds.

"I thought he was a robber!" Goat explains.

"A robber?"

"Yeah. I thought he was a robber. Stealing from you. From the store . . ."

"That's no robber. He's a sheriff. You killed him!"

Goat looks at his hand. At the peanut butter jar. At the sheriff, now lying in a pool of blood. "We gotta get outta here," he says.

Johnny suddenly springs into action.
As if he has been waiting for a moment like this.

He walks over to the sheriff and checks his pulse.

"He's still alive. Just knocked out," Johnny says.

Johnny rummages through the sheriff's clothes. He pulls out his wallet. His badge, radio, and handcuffs. He picks the gun up off the floor from near the sheriff's hand, and puts it in his own waistband. Then he rolls the sheriff over and cuffs him, hands behind his back.

Johnny stands up and pulls the gun out of his waistband. He hands it to Goat, who is now sitting on the floor. Blood is starting to permeate and infuse Goat's shirt around his stomach. He is looking pale. Johnny looks at the woman. "Don't move," he tells her.

She's not moving.

Johnny goes outside.

Opens back door of the car.

Gets roll of duct tape and rope.

Returns to store.

Sheriff is conscious now.

Goat is pointing the gun at the sheriff.

"Don't let him kill me," the sheriff pleads as Johnny walks in.

"He's not gonna kill you," Johnny says.

Johnny grabs the sheriff and drags him through the aisles to the bathroom.

He comes back out and looks at the woman.

He walks behind the counter.

"Put your hands behind your back," he tells her.

She complies.

Johnny unclips a key chain from her belt.

"Don't kill me, please," she says.

"We're not gonna kill you," Johnny replies.

Johnny tapes her hands together behind her back.

"Go to the bathroom, the men's," he orders her next.

She starts walking.

They get to the bathroom. Johnny opens the door.

She walks in.

"Sit down."

Johnny tapes her feet together. He tapes the sheriff's feet as well.

They are scared, but quiet.

They seem to realize Johnny is not going to hurt them.

They comply.

Then, in a web of rope and tape, he secures the two of them to the toilet.

He steps out of the bathroom.

He sees a circuit breaker on the wall.

He opens it and shuts off all the power to the property.

Goat speaks, "What are we doing? We need to get out of here."

"Working it," Johnny tells him.

Johnny walks outside and sees the sheriff's Blazer. He opens the driver's door. Then walks around to the other side and opens the passenger door.

He walks back into the store.

"What are we gonna do?" Goat asks.

"We're gonna get you to the best doctor in Mexico."

Johnny helps Goat stand up.
There is blood.
A lot of blood.
More blood than Johnny thought
possible.

Johnny helps Goat to the Blazer and loads
him into the passenger seat.

Johnny walks back inside.
Gets a mop from the back.
Cleans some of the blood from the floor.
Slides large welcome mat over
the remaining blood.

Steps out of the store.
Takes out the woman's keys.
Locks the door.

Gets in the Buick. Moves it next to the
Blazer. Transfers gear and loot into the Blazer.
Drives Buick around to the back of the store.
Runs back to the Blazer.

Gets in.
Starts it up.
Pulls out onto the highway.

JOCKO WILLINK

Picks
    up
        speed.

31

Maybe this wasn't a good call.
 Maybe I've made a mistake.
 Maybe I should try to undo it all.
 Maybe I should turn myself in.
 Or maybe
 This is all the way it is supposed to be.

"I can't believe I hit a cop with a fuckin' jar of peanut butter," Goat says, laughing, but his voice is weak.

"Remind me not to piss you off in the condiments section."

Goat laughs. But his laughter takes energy.

It makes him remember and realize what is actually happening.

Even though he doesn't know what is happening,

he knows what is happening.

"I'm bleedin' bad, Johnny."

"You're gonna be all right."

"I'm lucky I'm not bleeding fuckin' Cheez Whiz," Goat says. He chuckles. But his chuckle turns into a whimper.

Johnny laughs. "You're gonna be fine, Goat. You're gonna be okay."

32

"You know, Jessica, I'm not sure if Johnny is coming home tonight," Arty says.

"I was beginning to think the same thing." She pauses. Thinks. "But I really need to talk to him. Do you mind if I just wait for him?"

"Well, if you want, you can sleep in his room."

"Are you sure that would be all right?"

"Sure. You've slept there before a lot. I think it would be fine."

"Yeah, I guess so," Jessica replies, slightly embarrassed.

"Do you mind if I go to sleep?" Arty asks. "I have to go to work pretty early tomorrow."

"Of course, no problem."

Arty's face becomes suddenly excited as he asks, "If you have any laundry, I can take it with me tomorrow morning and clean it for you. Clean and press. I can bring it home in the afternoon. Or you can pick it up there at De Wasserette."

"That's okay, Arty. Alls I've got for clothes is these ones I'm wearin'. I'll be all right."

Arty is a little sad. But he's used to people not being as enthused as he is about laundry. "Okay. But if you change your mind, let me know."

"I will, Arty. And thanks for the tea. It's delicious."

"It is. It's Dutch. Pickwick," he says as he walks upstairs. "Oh, and good night."

"Good night, Arty."

Arty disappears up the stairs.
  Jessica finishes the tea.
    Washes the cup.
      Dries it.
        Puts it in the cabinet.

She heads up the stairs quietly.
  She opens the door to Johnny's room.
    Steps inside.

The light is on. She looks around.
  It's messy.
    But it's his.
      She feels his presence.

FINAL SPIN

In her heart.

Deeply.

Connected.

And she smiles.

33

Goat's eyes are shut.
   His breathing is slow.
      He's sleeping.
         Fading.

"GOAT! GOAT, WAKE UP! Don't go to sleep!"
Johnny shouts.

"I'm tired, man," Goat says in a feeble
voice. "I think I'm dying."

"I'm gonna take you to a hospital."

"How much further?"

"Not a Mexican hospital. An American one."

Goat suddenly speaks with more energy:
"Don't you fucking do that to me. You take
me with you. I'm going with you . . . señori-
tas . . ."

"No, man. No. You need a hospital. Now."

"Don't do it. I can make it. I can make
it . . ."

Goat passes out.

Johnny sees a sign ahead:

FINAL SPIN

NEXT EXIT
6 MILES

34

The manager, the officer, the guard, and the driver stand by the vault. The manager looks at his watch and counts down, "Five, four, three, two, one. That's it. Time delay is over. This should work . . ." He punches a code into the keypad.

Mechanical locks slide out of position.

He opens the door.

They look in.

They see Gerry. Taped up.

"Bastards," the manager mumbles.

"MMMmmmmMM," Gerry mumbles.

The officer walks by the manager. "Excuse me," he says, as he makes his way over to Gerry. The officer removes the tape from Gerry's head and face. It hurts him. He shows it. As soon as his mouth is clear, he speaks, "George Martinez and Jonathon MacDermott. They're the ones who did this. Little bastards."

"Yeah, I know," the manager replies. "The police are already after them. What happened?"

"They attacked me. They almost killed me. They tried to strangle me . . ."

"Why didn't you sound the alarm?" the manager asks.

"Look--I did the best I could. They ambushed me. I'm lucky to be alive, for Christ's sake."

"You'll be lucky to have a job," the manager says.

"But, sir! I . . . I was following procedures . . ."

"Were you?"

35

What did I do?
   What did I do?
   What did I do?
   What did I do?
   What did I do?
   What did I do?

"All right, man, we're almost there," Johnny tells Goat--and himself.

He coasts down the exit ramp from the highway.

"We're almost there, Goat. Goat? Goat! We're almost there. I'm takin' you to a hospital!"

The desert.
   Remote highway community.
      Strip malls.
      Empty streets.

Exit ramp comes to an end, hitting a road perpendicular.

Johnny looks both directions. He is sweating.

He sees more lights to the left. He heads in that direction.

As he turns, he yells. "GOAT! GOAT! Man, come on. Talk to me. Say something, man, say something."

Goat does not respond.

Johnny pulls to the side of the road.

He stops the Blazer. Gets out. Walks to the passenger side.

Opens the door.

"Goat," he says.

Goat does not respond.

Johnny grabs Goat's face and looks at it.

He shakes it.

He feels his neck for a pulse.

Nothing.

Whisper: "Goddamnit."

Louder: "Goddamnit, Goat."

Whisper: "Goddamnit."

Johnny buries his head in Goat's chest.

He weeps. "I'm sorry, man. I'm sorry. Goddam-nit, I'm sorry, Goat."

He sobs for a minute.
　　Then he gets himself together.
　　He stands up straight and shuts the door.
　　He walks back to the driver's side, gets in, starts the engine, and drives down the road.
　　He sees a pay phone. Outside a saloon. Saloon is closed.

　　Stops.
　　　　Gets out.
　　　　　　Coins into phone.
　　　　　　Dials.

"Hello?" Arty says in a groggy voice.
"Arty. It's me."
"Hi, Johnny. Where are you?"
"Look, Arty. I did something. Something bad. I . . . I'm not gonna be coming home again."
"Where are you going?"
"I don't know. But I wanted to tell you that

you are all set. If you need anything, ask Mr. Vossen. He is going to take care of you."

"When are you coming back?"

"I don't know. I don't know. But I want you to know you're all set, Arty. You've got nothing to worry about. I took care of everything-- me and Goat did." Johnny's voice cracks from the emotion.

"You always take care of me."

"Well, now you're gonna have to take care of yourself, okay? Now I've got to get going."

"Jessica is here," Arty says.

"What?" Johnny says, surprised.

"Jessica is here. She was looking for you and she stayed here."

"What? What does she want?"

"She said she needed to talk to you."

"To talk to me?"

"Yes, Johnny. She's here. She said she needs to talk to you. I gave her some Pick- wick tea."

"And she's still there, now? Right now?"

"She is. She is asleep in your room."

"Can you get her for me?"

"Yes, I can. Hold on."

Johnny lowers his head. He waits. He looks around.

"Hello?"

Jessica says.
She sounds like an angel.

A damn angel.

"Jess? It's me."
   "I know it's--"
   "I got some shit to tell you. I fucked up.
Me and Goat--"

   "I'm pregnant."

Silence.

"What?"

         "I'm pregnant."

Silence.

"When did you find out?"
   "This afternoon."
   "Why didn't you call me?" Johnny asks.
   "I wanted to tell you to your face. When
you got home."
   Silence.

152

"I'm not mad," she says quietly. "I'm actually not mad at all."

"I'm not mad at all either. Not at all."

For a moment:

> There is promise and hope and
> joy and life.

Johnny feels a warmth come over him.
    He closes his eyes.
        He begins to feel

                happy.

He opens his eyes.
    Blood on his hands.

"Look," he says, "I'm in a lot of trouble. A lot."

    "I know," Jessica says, "the police called here. What did you--"

    "The police called there? When?"

    "An hour . . . maybe hour and a half ago. What did you do?"

    "Goat's dead."

    "Goat's dead?"

    "Yeah. He is. I'm on the run. I'm headed . . . I'm headed out."

"Are you coming back?"

"I don't think I'll be able to. If I do, I'm going to jail."

"Fuck."

"I'm sorry, Jess. I'm so sorry. I . . . I just didn't know."

"What am I going to do now?" she asks.

Johnny listens.

He thinks.

He sees.

His tone changes.

"Jessica. Listen. Stay at my house. Wait by the phone. Don't go to work. Don't go anywhere. I will call you. Trust me. I'm sorry. But you have to trust me now."

"What are you going to do?"

"I'm going to take care of you. You and Arty. I'll call you. Don't tell anyone."

"Don't tell anyone about what?"

"About anything. About me. That you talked to me. About the baby. Nothing. Don't say anything. Just wait. I'll call you . . . okay?"

"Okay."

"I'll talk to you soon."
"Okay."
"Okay."
"Bye."
"Bye."

Johnny hangs up the phone. He walks over to
the Blazer, gets in, and speeds off.
He gets back on the highway.

                    He's on a mission.

Jessica hangs up the phone. She puts her head
in her hands.

    She's not crying--
        in the sense that no tears are leaving
        her eyes.

                    But she is in anguish.

36

Got to make this work.
Make something good of this.
All of this.
Of me.
For them.

The Blazer roars down the highway.
Goat's body, slumped in the front seat.

Dead.

Bags of money in the back seat.

Full.

Johnny sees a sign:

EXIT 27

He scans the area.
Remote desert.
No signs of life.

He takes the exit.
    Drives.
    Barren area.
    Right turn.
    Left turn.
    Long straight road.
    Straight.
    Straight ahead.
    Reaches a four-way intersection.
    Stops.
    Gets out.
    Reads the street signs marking the roads
at intersection.
    "Buell and Bonnet," he whispers to himself.
    Walks to side of road.
    Looks left. Looks right.
    He is alone.

    All alone.

He sees what he is looking for: drainage ditch
that leads to a pipe that goes under the road.

    This will work.
    He walks back over to the Blazer.
    Pulls out the duffel bags. He checks the
    zippers.
        Opens them slightly.

Confirms the money is there.
Grabs two stacks. Thumbs through
them. Puts the two stacks in
his jacket pocket.
  Zips the duffel bags tightly
  back up.
    Leaves the hatch of the
    Blazer open.

He walks back to the drainage ditch.
  Follows it to the pipe that goes under
  the road.
    Sets down the bags.

He pulls some debris out of the pipe.
  Sticks.
    Trash.

Once clear, Johnny shoves the duffel bags
into the pipe.
  Deep.
Then he places all the debris he pulled out
in front of the bags.
  Camouflage.
He steps back.
  No one will find that.
He looks at the sky. It is clear. The stars
are bright. He smiles at them.

I hope the weather holds.
He walks back to the Blazer.
Looks at the street signs again.
    Buell and Bonnet
    Buell and Bonnet

He walks to the passenger door.
    Opens it.
        He looks at Goat.

Pale.
        Cold.
                Lifeless.

Johnny carefully lifts him out of the seat
and carries him to the back of the Blazer.

        Slowly lays him down.

        He looks:

            peaceful.

Johnny takes a step back.
    Studies Goat for a few seconds.
    Shuts hatch.
    Gets in Blazer.

        Drives off.

37

The policeman is sitting in his cruiser just off the side of an open stretch of highway.

In the distance: headlights.

They seem to be moving fast.

Damn, he thinks.

He pulls the trigger on the radar gun.

A few moments pass.

It registers: 94.

"Son-of-a-bitch," he says to himself.

He puts the radar gun away. Puts his seat belt on. Waits for the vehicle to pass him.

It blows by.

Johnny sees the police cruiser as he passes it.

"No! Damnit."

Johnny checks his rearview mirror.

> Hoping,
>> wishing,
>>> praying that the police car does not pull out.

But it does.
Johnny accelerates.
But the Blazer cannot outrun the cruiser.
Cruiser gains on Johnny.
Cruiser pulls alongside the Blazer.
Johnny looks over.
The policeman is motioning to Johnny to pull over.

Johnny looks forward again and accelerates, pulling ahead of the cruiser.
Lights and sirens come on.
The cruiser pulls up beside Johnny again.

The policeman once again motions to pull over.
Johnny stares straight ahead.

"Goddamnit," the policeman says, again speaking to himself.

He was not in the mood for this.
It was late.
He was tired.
His shift was almost over.
Now this.

Should have just let him go, he thinks.

Too late for that.

The policeman accelerates past the Blazer.
Pulls in front.

Johnny shifts to the left.
The cruiser blocks him.
He shifts to the right.
The cruiser blocks him.

Johnny pushes down the gas and nudges gently into the cruiser.
Sending a message.
Then he shifts to the left.

The cruiser blocks him.
He shifts to the right.
The cruiser blocks him.
Message not received.
No time for this.
No choice.
Go time.

Johnny floors the gas pedal and smashes into the rear quarter panel of the cruiser.

FINAL SPIN

It fishtails, spins out of control, off the road, flips several times, and comes to a rest.

Johnny slows down.
    Comes to a stop.
        He looks in his rearview mirror.
           Sees the vehicle. Smoking.
            Turns around and looks.
           It looks bad.

He puts the Blazer in reverse and backs up until he is parallel with the cruiser.

He opens his door. Leaves engine running. Gets out.

Walks over to the cruiser, which is sitting upright, but is severely damaged.

"Hey! You all right?" Johnny yells.

Silence.

He tries again. "Hey! You all right? I'm not gonna hurt you. Just don't shoot me. Are you okay?"

"My shoulder is broken," the policeman finally responds.

"Can you get out of the car?"

"I think . . . if I could get to the seat belt."

"I'll help you. But don't shoot at me."

"I won't. I won't. Just give me a hand, please."

Johnny slowly makes his way closer to the cruiser.

He sees that the policeman is immobilized. Trapped. His face is bleeding. Johnny gets closer. Peers inside.

"I can't move my right arm," the policeman says.

"Okay. I'll get you out. Okay?"

"Okay."

"Don't shoot me," Johnny says again.

"I won't. Just get me out of here."

Johnny reaches in the car through the window. Reaches across the policeman. He feels his holster by the seat belt fastener. He pulls out the officer's pistol.

"Hey! Hey!" The policeman shouts, now scared, "Don't shoot me."

"I'm not gonna shoot you. I'm not gonna."

Johnny puts the pistol in his waistband. He reaches inside the cruiser again and grabs the mic of the radio on the policeman's collar and the one attached to the radio mounted in the cruiser and rips them both out.

"What are you doing?" the policeman asks.

"Just need you to stay quiet for a bit," Johnny responds.

"I already called it in," the policeman says.

"No you didn't. I got a radio in the Blazer. I woulda heard."

The policeman nods, defeated.

Johnny reaches in again, this time unfastening the policeman's seat belt.

He opens the door of the car and steps back.

"All right. Looks like you're gonna be okay. I gotta go," Johnny says.

"You gonna leave me here?" the policeman asks.

"Yes, I am. I'm sure someone will find you soon enough."

"They are going to find you too," the policeman says.

"I know. I know."

Johnny walks back to the Blazer. He sees steam escaping from the front. He walks to inspect. It's obvious: hitting the cruiser damaged the radiator.

It's leaking.

Bad.

"Damnit," he says. He gets back in the Blazer and takes off down the highway.

The sun is coming up.

38

I can't make it much farther.
I have to figure this out.

Steam bellowing.
    Heat indicator: pegged.
Passes a sign:

EXIT 13

He slowly passes the ramp.
The highway cuts through a very small town.
Mostly abandoned buildings.
Remote.
Perfect.
Stop.

    Reverse.
      Take exit.

All is as it appeared.

Abandoned highway town.

FINAL SPIN

Dilapidated buildings.
Deserted lots.
Forsaken streets.

He drives around.
Some run-down houses.
A small convenience store.
Pay phone out front.

He sees an old service station down the street. Abandoned.
That should work.
He pulls the Blazer in.

Shuts it down and gets out.
Peers into the windows.
Dark.
Grease stains.
Neglected tools.
Dust and grime.
Abandoned.

Still early in the morning.
Looks up and down the street: empty.
Picks up small rock.
Smashes small window. Unlocks door. Opens it.
Meanders through the building into the repair bays.

Opens one of the garage doors.
Walks out.
Gets in Blazer.
Starts it.
Drives it into repair bay.
Gets out.
Shuts garage door.

Looks at his watch: 6:42.

Steps outside and walks to the pay phone.
Digs some change out of his pocket. Inserts. Dials. Rings.
"Hello?" Arty answers.
"Arty. It's me."
"Hi, Johnny. Are you in trouble? Jessica said you were in some kind of trouble?"
"A little bit, Arty. A little bit. But don't worry about me. Is Jessica there?"
"She is. Do you want to talk to her?"
"Yes, please, Arty. Please."
"Okay. Hold on."
Silence.
"Wait," Arty says, "there's someone here. Someone banging on the door."
"Let me talk to him," Jessica says in the background, sounding panicked. Then she is loud and clear: "The cops are here."

"At the house?"

"Yes, here. They are banging on the door. They are coming in."

"Into the house?"

"I'm going. We'll talk later," Jessica says.

"All right," says Johnny. He hangs up.

She will handle it.
She's that kind of girl.

Johnny walks back toward the garage.

Nervous. Angry. Focused.

Enters garage. Opens Blazer door and starts to inspect it. Finds a flashlight. Shines the flashlight at the shotgun rack bolted into the dash, with shotgun. It is locked. Pulls out the sheriff's keys. Third one works. Takes out shotgun. Sets it on hood of Blazer. Goes back inside Blazer and reaches under the seat, pulls out the pistol he had taken from the sheriff. Places it on the hood as well. Goes back again and finds ammunition for both weapons. Loads the shotgun. Loads the pistol.

Ready.

For what?

39

Two deputies in a police cruiser pull into the parking lot of Frannie's on the interstate.

They see the Buick.

Things are quiet.

This is their territory. They know that it is normally lit up with at least some activity.

Makes them: suspicious.

One of the deputies calls in the license plate.

"This is Victor two-five out at Frannie's Grill on the interstate. I need you to run a plate for me. Seven, two, Adam, Mary, ocean, niner. From a blue early eighties Buick Century wagon."

"10-4. I read back: seven, two, Adam, Mary, ocean, niner? Is that solid?"

"10-4."

"And you're looking at an early eighties Buick Century wagon?"

"Affirmative."

"Stand by."

Silence.

"Victor two-five, this is dispatch."

"Go for two-five."

"Roger. Be advised, there is a statewide APB out on that vehicle. One white male, one Mexican. Robbery suspects. Early twenties. Consider armed and dangerous."

"Copy that. We're initiating a 10-59 on this."

"Good copy, 10-59. Let us know what you need."

One of the deputies exits the vehicle.

Looks around the front of the store.

Shines his flashlight in the window.

Sees remnants of blood that has been wiped across the floor.

He keys the radio mic on his lapel.

"This is Victor two-five. Request immediate backup. Immediate backup, Frannie's Grill, rest stop, exit thirty-eight."

"This is dispatch. 10-4. Backup requested at Frannie's Grill at the rest stop off exit thirty-eight. Will have units inbound directly."

The deputy looks down at his feet.

Sees more blood on the ground.

Had enough.

He pulls the baton off his duty belt and smashes the door-window. He replaces the baton, then draws his weapon and flashlight and enters the building.

Sees the light switch on the wall. Flips it up and down. Nothing.

Pans the room with his flashlight. No movement.

Then: noise.

Muffled voice from the back of the shop.

Cautiously, he moves toward the back, his gun and flashlight trained in the direction of the voice.

"MMMmmmm. MmmmmmmMM."

The sound is coming from the men's bathroom door.

The deputy listens for a moment.

Then, he kicks the door open.

He scans the room from outside.

Sees two bodies on the floor, obviously bound.

He makes entry into the room, clears it, then holsters his weapon and sets his flashlight on the ground and starts untying and untaping the woman. Then he looks at the sheriff. He recognizes him. He is shocked.

As he gets the sheriff untaped, the sheriff speaks: "Give me your radio."

"My radio?"

"Yes. Your radio. Let me call this in."

"Here you go, Sheriff."

The sheriff keys the mic. "All stations this net, all stations this net, this is Oscar-one. I'm issuing an APB on a dark green unmarked Chevy Blazer, license plate Adam, yellow, yellow, two, Adam, two. Suspects one white male, early twenties. One Mexican male, early twenties. Mexican suspect is wounded in the stomach from attempted robbery. Assumed to be headed south toward the border. Suspects to be considered armed and dangerous."

"Copy that, Oscar-One. Dispatch is standing by."

The sheriff looks at the woman. "Can you get the lights back on in here?"

"Yes, sir, Sheriff," she replies, and she makes her way to the circuit panel.

"And can I use your telephone?" the sheriff asks.

"Sure. It's up here by the register."

She leads him to the front.

The sheriff rubs his head.

It aches.

At the counter, he picks up the phone. Dials. Waits.

"Yeah. Patch me through to the chief. I know he's sleeping. Patch me through. This is Sheriff Townsend and I need to speak to him

immediately. Immediately. Thank you." He is
quiet for a moment, then begins again, "Rob,
this is Mike Townsend from up north. We have
a situation. I got attacked and knocked out. I
shot one of them in the gut, but they got the
upper hand and stole my gun. They also stole
my vehicle. I already put an APB on it, but I'm
gonna need more support so I can track these
sons-a-bitches down. There's a lot of country
to cover, and they must be heading to the border. We have to cut them off. All right. Yes,
all right. Thanks for the help. No, I'll be
all right. Thanks. Thanks for the help. 10-4.
Out." He hangs up the phone and then looks at
the deputy. "We'll have these bastards wrapped
up in no time."

His call with the chief puts a string of
events in motion.
    Extra officers recalled to duty.
      Roadblocks.
      Helicopters.

      Manhunt.

40

Just need to keep it together.
  Figure it out.
  For Arty.
  For Jessica.
  For the baby.

For Goat.

Johnny opens the hatch to the Blazer.
  He sees Goat.
  He finds some old plastic tarps.
  Lays them out behind the Blazer.
  Eases Goat's body out of the Blazer and onto the tarps.
        Rolls him up in the tarps.
          Stares at him.

Sorry, Goat. I'm sorry.

Johnny starts thinking about how to repair the Blazer. He begins gathering tools, spare parts, and other assorted items he thinks

might be of help. He refills the radiator.
It's leaking, but he figures in a pinch, he
could get some miles out of her.

He wants to fix things.

But want doesn't do much good.

41

"We need to know where he is if we are going to be able to help him," a detective says.

"I am sorry, but he is not here," responds Arty, sitting at their kitchen table. Jessica looks on.

"When was the last time you heard from him?" the detective asks.

"Not too long ago. He called."

"He called?"

"Yes. He called. On the phone."

"Did he say where he is? Or where he is going?"

"He didn't say where he was. He didn't say where he was going. Except for, he said he wasn't coming back."

The detective looks at Jessica. "And you are?"

"I'm his friend," she says, pointing at Arty.

Arty smiles.

"She's my friend."

"What are you doing up so late?" the detective asks. "We saw lights on when we pulled up."

"Drinking tea," Jessica says.

"Tea?" the detective says.

"Tea. Pickwick tea. It's from Holland," Arty tells the detective. "Do you want me to make you a cup?"

The detective looks puzzled. "No, thank you."

42

Sheriff station.
    Desks.
        Cubicles.
            Briefing room.
            Map.

The sheriff is standing, looking at a map of Southern California and Arizona.

The border with Mexico is prominent.

"I think they might have stopped. That CHP officer said he could have damaged the Blazer when they PIT'd him," the sheriff says.

"No guarantee of that," one of the officers replies.

"Well also, one of them is bleeding out. Gut-shot. They might have tried to hole up somewhere. Border Patrol doesn't have a match going across the border heading south. That's not gonna be perfect, but they had a look at CCT. No Blazers."

Silence as the group assembles this information in their minds.

"You s'pose they could have made it to the Salton Sea?" one officer asks.

"Judging from the time they hit the CHP officer and now, yeah, I'd say that's a good place to start."

"So how do you want to do it?"

"I recommend we start teams on the south end and roll up the east and west sides on the 111 and the 86. Look for the Blazer. And anything else."

"Makes sense, Sheriff."

"All right then, let's execute. It's seven twenty right now. We should be able to get this up and running by seven forty-five, eight at the latest."

Radio calls go out.

Police officers, Sheriff's Department, Border Patrol, and other government law enforcement organizations get the word.

They roll out.
Looking.
Seeking.

43

Two police cruisers slowly make their way down the street.

Scanning.

They roll by abandoned buildings.

Deserted shops.

Then a small convenience store.

They pull up to the shop and go in.

They ask the attendant: "Seen anyone?" "Heard anything?" "Know anything?"

Nothing. Nada.

One of the officers walks around outside the convenience store.

Around the back.

Checks the dumpsters.

He's a curious one.

He walks over to the pay phone outside.

It's dusty.

But it has handprints on it.

Fresh handprints.

"Bill!" he yells to one of the other officers. "Come check this out."

Bill casually strolls over.

"Look at these fresh handprints. Someone made a call. First one in a while too."

"Yep. Have the perps made any calls that we know of?"

"Yep. Report said one of them called his brother earlier. Couple hours ago."

"Damn. They could be here."

"Let's go, boys. We need to scour this place."

They load back into their cruisers and begin to patrol through the village.

Dust.

    Dirt.

        Garbage.

            Dilapidation.

                A few houses, trailers, shops.

They roll by the garage where Johnny is holed up.

One of the officers notices the broken window.

There is some glass on the ground.

Looks fresh.

"Hold up. Take a look at that window. Freshly broken."

Johnny sees them outside. He is in the open and freezes.

He moves behind the Blazer. His movement is detected.

"Somebody's in there!" one of the officers shouts.

"You think it's the guys?"

"Looks like there's a vehicle in there too. Could be the Blazer."

"Let's go get 'em."

"Hold what you got. No reason to rush here. Let me get some backup."

One of the officers picks up his radio mic and says, "This is unit nine. We've got a possible sighting of the fugitives. Out here at Desert Shores off the 86. Request immediate backup."

Johnny watches stealthily through the windows of the Blazer and the garage as the officer makes the radio call.

Knows they must be calling for backup.

He looks at his watch. Nine forty-eight.

I've got to get out of here.

Now.

He puts the shotgun in the Blazer across the passenger seat.

He looks at the garage door, assessing if he can smash through it with the Blazer.

But the door is a heavy industrial door. He's not sure he can make it through.

Gonna have to open it.

He inspects the mechanism. Understands how to open it.

Rehearses it a few times in his mind.

Walks back over to the Blazer.

Starts it up.

In the early desert-morning air, the engine starting sounds like an eruption.

"That's him!" one of the officers shouts.

"We can't be sure yet," another yells.

The garage door begins to open.

They hit the lights on the cruisers and maneuver the vehicles into a better position, both facing the garage door. One of the officers picks up the PA mic and starts talking.

"Stay where you are. This is the police. I repeat: Stay where you are."

One of the other officers opens his passenger-side door, drops to a knee, and takes aim on the garage door.

"DO NOT MOVE!" the PA announces sternly.

Johnny has thrown the garage door all the way open. He gets into the Blazer.

"MOVING THAT VEHICLE WILL RESULT IN THE USE OF LETHAL FORCE. EXIT THE VEHICLE NOW!"

Now or never.

Johnny puts the Blazer into gear. As soon as he does, two of the officers open fire. One with a pistol, the other with a shotgun.

Windshield: hit.
   Engine: hit.
      Tires: hit.
         Radiator: hit.

HIT. HIT. HIT. HIT.

Johnny ducks down. The engine sputters.

"SHOTS FIRED! SHOTS FIRED!" one of the officers yells into his radio.

HIT. HIT.

Bullets rip through the Blazer. The engine shuts down.

Johnny jumps out of the Blazer and dives behind the protection of the garage walls.

He scurries to the chain that controls the garage door and yanks it down. The garage door shuts.

"UNIT NINE! NEED IMMEDIATE BACKUP. Desert Shores. Corner of Mountain View and Monterey streets. We've got the suspects. We've got the

suspects. SHOTS FIRED! SHOTS FIRED!" an officer yells into his radio.

"10-4, unit nine. Sending units your way
at this time."

Johnny sits.

Blood trickles from his face where shards
of glass cut him.

But he's still alive.

I can make this work.

44

Johnny looks at his watch. 11:48.

He has been listening to all kinds of activity outside.

He can catch glimpses of what is taking place.

The law is everywhere.

Police cars.
SWAT vehicles.

Surrounded.

This will work.
This will work.
I can make this work.
They'll never know.

The commotion and bustle settles down.

Things get quiet.

A PA speaker breaks the silence. "All right. Jonathon. George. Listen up. We know who you are. We know what you did. We want to work this out. You haven't killed anyone. It's just a bad day. Don't let it get worse."

Just a bad day?
What about the previous twenty years?

"I want to bring you a phone so we can talk to you. So we can figure this out. If that is okay, just tap on the window so we can hear you."

Johnny scurries around the floor and finds a broomstick. From his position behind a wall he taps the window.

"Okay. Perfect." The PA continues, "Now. My man here is gonna walk up to the front door. He is unarmed. Unarmed, okay. Just a guy doing his job. Putting himself at risk to try and help you. All he has is the phone. He'll set it down next to the door there. Okay. Right in a nice spot so you can grab it, okay? If that's okay, tap the window twice again."

Johnny taps the window.

"Okay. Great. See--we can work this out. Just take it easy. This is going to be fine. I'm sending my man now."

The negotiator motions to one of the deputies, then points at the garage.

One of the deputies slowly makes his way toward the garage.

Lays out phone wire behind him.
Gets to door.
Kneels.
    Sets down phone.
        Nudges it close to the door.
Slowly walks away, back to skirmish line
of police and their vehicles.

"All right, guys. The phone is by the front
door. You are free to go to the door, open it,
and pick up the phone. Then you can bring it
back inside so you are comfortable. No big
deal. I just want to be able to talk to you so
we can figure this out."

Johnny crawls over to the door. It's the
front door, not the one he entered earlier.

Glass with metal frame.
    Push bar across the middle.

He pushes the door to open it.

    It is locked.
    Does not move.

He crawls back to the service area and
grabs an old wrench.
    Back to the door.
        He taps the glass a few times.

189

The negotiator sees this. He understands what is happening. He keys the mic on his radio and says, "Hold your fire. Hold your fire. He's going to break the glass to get the phone. HOLD YOUR FIRE."

Then he keys the PA system. "All right, guys. The door is locked and you want to break the glass. That's fine. All my officers know what you are doing. Go ahead and break the glass."

Even though no one can see him, Johnny nods.

Here we go.

He smashes the glass.

Police officers train their weapons on the door.

Johnny reaches his hand from behind the wall, feels the ground, gets ahold of the phone, and brings it back behind the wall.

Johnny sits with his back to the wall.

He lifts the phone receiver to his ear and says, "Hello?"

"Just a minute," an officer says, and then yells, "Got him on the line!"

The negotiator walks over to the phone. Officer hands it to him.

"Jonathon?"

"Yep."

"How ya doing in there?"

"Not so good. How about you?"

"Well--things could be better. You made a bit of a mess out here."

"I know."

"But it's nothing we can't fix. You assaulted a plain-clothed sheriff. But he's gonna be okay. And that highway patrol officer you hit. He got a little dinged up--his shoulder is hurt pretty bad. But he's gonna be okay too. And we know you helped him out. So we are all okay over here. But what about you? And what about your buddy, George? We know he's been shot. And let me tell you, a gut-shot like he has is not a good thing. If we don't get him some help, it could get--"

"He's dead."

Silence.

"I'm sorry about that, Jonathon."

"Don't be. It's my fault."

"Let's not worry about that right now. Let's worry about you. Let's get you out of this situation. Why don't you come on out of there so we can get this situation all worked out."

"Nah," Johnny says, "I'm not coming out just yet."

"Come on, Jonathon. The longer you sit in there, the more tense everyone gets. There's no reason for that. Plus it's hot out here. We don't want to be sitting out here any more than you want to be sitting in there."

"You're gonna have to give me a little more time."

"How much time we talking about, Jonathon?" the negotiator asks.

"I don't know. Let me just think through this thing."

"Okay, okay. It's gonna be fine. We can wait if you need time. You hungry? Want some food?"

"Yeah, sure. I'll take some food. What do ya got?"

"How 'bout some donuts? I can get you some donuts."

"Sounds good. Send me some donuts. I'm gonna take a break."

"Don't hang up, Johnny. Tell me what else you want."

"I want a break," Johnny says as he hangs up the phone.

The SWAT team leader has been listening.

"We should take him down," he says to the negotiator.

"Not yet. He'll come around."

"I don't think so. He's already tried to murder two police. We need to take him."

"Just let me work it, okay? Please?"

"Fine. But we can't give him too much time. He could be in there setting up on us. The more time we give him, the more set up he will be. Don't put my guys at risk."

45

Time to do this.
  Figure it out.
  Make this all work out.

Johnny crawls around the garage.

  Gathering things.
    Old piece of hose.
      Rags.
        Buckets and other containers.

  He drags them over to the car.
  Rear quarter panel. Passenger side. Where
the gas cap is.

  Opens gas cap cover.
    Removes gas cap.
      Inserts hose.
  Sucks gas into the hose.
    Forms siphon.
      Spits.

Begins filling containers and buckets with gas.

Once they are all filled with gas, he removes the hose from the gas tank.
This will go up like a torch.
No one will figure it out.
Johnny slides away from the gas and puts his back up against the wall.
He thinks through it.
"Gonna deliver you those donuts now, Jonathon," the negotiator says over the PA. "Pick up the phone."
Johnny crawls over to the phone and picks it up. "Hey."
"Just want to bring you those donuts you wanted. Can I send my man up there again?"
"Yeah. Fine. Send him up."
The negotiator motions to the deputy, who proceeds slowly to the door.
Sets down box of donuts.
Walks away slowly.
"There you go, Jonathon. There's some donuts for you."
Johnny hangs up the phone. Reaches slowly outside the door.
Grabs box.

Opens.
    Grabs donut.
        Eats.
            Waits.

This is going to work.

"Pick up the phone, Jonathon. I need to talk to you."

Johnny looks at his watch. 2:40.

He looks at the phone.

"I've got something else here for you."

Silence.

"Jonathon. Pick up the phone. Come on."

Johnny crawls over to the phone and picks it up. "What's up?" he asks.

"I want you to take a look out the window."

"Why? So you can get a good shot at me?"

"No, Jonathon. That's not it at all. I've got something I want you to see. Take a look. Please."

Johnny pauses. Makes his way to the window. Slowly lifts his head.

It is his first full view of the scene.

He scans the area looking in the direction of the PA system. He sees

a squad car. The negotiator is standing
there, staring at him.
Standing next to him are Arty and Jessica.

Johnny's head involuntarily raises so he
can get a better view.
He gets a good look at them.

Arty looks nervous.
Jessica looks nervous too.
But also, at the same time, confident.

She's got this.
Strong woman.

Johnny realizes he is exposed.
Drops to the ground.
Picks up phone.

"What the hell are they doing here?" he
asks.
"They just want to talk to you, Jonathon.
They want you to come out."
"Let me talk to my brother."
"Fine, Jonathon. He can talk some sense
into you."
The negotiator passes the phone to Arty.

"Johnny?"

"Hey, Arty. You okay?"

"I'm fine, Johnny. I brought you a change of clothes."

"Thanks, Arty."

"The police told me I should tell you to come out."

"I'm going to come out, Arty. I just need a few minutes. Tell them to calm down. I'll be out soon."

"Why don't you just come out now? So we can go home?"

"In a bit, Arty. In a bit. Can you let me talk to Jessica?"

"Sure."

"He wants to talk to her," Arty says to the negotiator as he motions toward Jessica.

The negotiator takes the phone. He covers the microphone and says to her, "You get him to come out or we're going in, okay?" He hands her the phone.

"Okay," Jessica says to the negotiator. She takes the phone. "Johnny?"

"Hey, Jess. How ya doin'?"

"Shitty. How about you?"

"Same."

"You need to come out of there, Johnny."

"I'm going to. I'll be out soon."

"If you don't come out, they're coming in."

"I know."

"Then come out. Just come out."

"I will. I told you, I will."

Silence.

"I'm sorry, Johnny."

"Why? You've got nothing to be sorry for. You made me happy."

"If I'd have called you and told you, you wouldn't have gotten into all this shit."

"Maybe, Jess. Maybe. But it's all right. Everything is going to be okay."

The negotiator interrupts. "Let me talk to him."

"The cop wants to talk to you again."

"All right. But hey--it's gonna be okay."

"Okay."

Jessica hands the phone to the negotiator.

"Jonathon--this has gone on long enough. I need you to come out of there."

"I know you do. I'm going to."

Johnny hangs up the phone.

46

All right. Been a good run.
   So I get some jail time.
   What? Three years? Five?
   I'll figure it out.
   Jessica will be there.
   This will take care of her.
                And the baby.
   Arty will be fine for a few years too.
   The laundromat.
   Jessica can help him.
   Everything's going to be fine.
   Just need to get this over with.
   Do my time.
          For them.
            Here we go.

Johnny crawls back to the gas cap of the Blazer.
   Takes rags and rips them up.
     Ties them together, end to end.
       Long strip.
         Soaks in gas in one of the buckets.

200

Stuffs one end of it into the fuel filler pipe.

Other end drapes to the floor.

"Bring over Mike!" the police captain shouts.

"We need more time, Captain," the negotiator responds.

"It's been long enough."

Mike, the SWAT team commander, arrives.

"We going?"

"We need more time, Mike." The negotiator repeats himself.

"The longer we wait, the more stressed he gets. The more stressed he gets, the more unpredictable this is."

"We don't want that," the captain agrees.

"Look, no, we don't want that. But we also don't want a gunfight. Let me work on this guy. He's not some damn career criminal. He hasn't killed anyone. He's a damn kid."

"A kid that ran an officer off the road!" the captain shouts.

"And then went back to make sure he was okay!"

"What about the sheriff he assaulted?"

"With a jar of peanut butter! Come on. He's in over his head. Let me give him an out."

"Assault is assault," the captain says, "and this guy is in the wrong. We need to take him down. Mike, have your guys get their gear on."

"Roger that, boss," the SWAT team leader says.

He walks back to his team, who await his command.

"Get it on."

The team pick up their helmets, weapons, and body armor.

"And get your masks ready. We are going to soften him up a bit. Rob, load up a gas canister and be ready to put one right through that window."

"Roger that," a SWAT team member replies.

The team get out their gas masks and begin final preparations with their gear.

The SWAT leader walks back over to the captain.

"Making final preps right now."

"Good."

"We should hold off. I'm telling you," the negotiator pleads.

"Well, I'm telling you, we aren't holding

off anymore." The captain looks at the SWAT team leader. "It's time."

"Got it. I'm gonna soften him up--hit him with some tear gas."

"You really think you need to?" asks the captain.

"He's been in there all day. Hasn't slept all night. He's got weapons. He's cornered. He's already attacked police officers. Yes. We need to."

The captain considers this. "All right," he says. "All right."

"Just give me a chance," the negotiator says.

"You had your chance," the captain tells him. He looks at the SWAT leader. "You know what to do. Make it happen."

"Roger that," the SWAT team leader replies. He walks away, toward his team.

"You just keep him talking," the captain says to the negotiator.

The negotiator exhales deeply. "Will do . . . will do."

He speaks over the PA.

"Need to talk to you, Johnny. Pick up the phone."

Johnny crawls over and picks it up.

"What's up?"

"Just checking in. Your brother and your girl want to know what you are thinking."

"I'm thinking I'm pretty thirsty."

47

The SWAT team leader gets back to his troops.
Brings them together.

Sketches the target building in the sand.

Briefs them on The Plan.

"Rob, you get over here by the end of our vehicles," he says, pointing at the dirt map. "We are going to approach from over here on the red side. He won't be able to see us because of the dead space. We are going to enter through the front door. When I give the execute, I want you to put the gas right through the window on the white side. You got it, Rob?"

"Got it."

The SWAT team leader continues: "Breach team, once that gas goes in, he'll be distracted. Forrest"--he looks at a young, thin, and nervous new SWAT team member--"you hold security for the breach team. You're going to be number one man." The SWAT leader looks up at Forrest.

One of the other members of the team slaps him on the back. "Cherry boy! Number one man! GET SOME!" he shouts.

"Okay, okay. We were all new guys at some point. You good with this, Forrest?"

"Yes, sir," Forrest responds anxiously.

"Okay. So, like I was saying, once the gas hits, Forrest on point, hold security on the front door so the breach team can do their thing. Breach team--standard deal. Set it, blast it. When it goes, we go. From there we all know what to do. Any questions?" the SWAT leader asks as he looks over his team from man to man. "No questions? All right then. We go."

The SWAT team begins to move into their position, hidden by police vehicles.

"You know, it's getting pretty hot out here," the negotiator says over the phone, "what do you say we call it a day?"

"Sounds like a good idea. I'll tell you what, let me just finish this do--"

Johnny is cut off by the sound of breaking glass as a gas canister smashes through the window. He looks into the garage. He sees the canister spin across the floor.

It comes to a stop by the buckets of gasoline and the rags going into the fuel tank of the Blazer. There is a pop as its ignition fires.

The ignition creates a spark.
The gas bursts into flames.
Johnny sees the fire.

The SWAT team is moving into position.
The fire starts to climb the cloth toward the gas tank of the Blazer.
Johnny sees it, almost as if in slow motion.

This thing is going to blow.

He stands up and charges for the front door, trying to escape.
Breaks the doorjamb.
Barrels through the door.

Forrest, startled, fires a shot into Johnny.

The bullet hits him square in the chest.

Johnny falls to the ground.

The SWAT team begins to enter the now open front door.

"It's gonna blow!" one man shouts as he sees the fire and the fuel. "RETREAT!"

The SWAT team bails out of the building.

One of the members grabs Johnny by the foot and drags him away from the building.

"MEDIC!"
one SWAT member yells.

The fire reaches the Blazer's fuel tank.
Fire explodes.
Lashes out of windows.
Crawls up walls.

Engulfs building.

The SWAT members continue to run away from the building, dragging Johnny.

Jessica runs toward the building.
Arty follows.

At a safe distance, the SWAT team member dragging Johnny stops and kneels down, inspecting his wound.

FINAL SPIN

"MEDIC!"

In the chaos, Jessica moves toward Johnny.

A police officer starts to stop her. He looks at her. Looks at Johnny. He can see Johnny is in rough shape: not a threat. He lets Jessica go to Johnny.

> She kneels down next to him.
>> Brushes his face with her hand.
> Arty arrives.
>> Watches.

"Johnny . . ."

"I'm sorry, Jess."

"Are you going to be okay, Johnny?" Arty asks.

"I don't think so, buddy."

"You're gonna be fine," Jessica says.

"No. I don't think so, Jess. But you guys are. All of you." Johnny smiles weakly, and looks at her stomach. "You're gonna be okay."

"No, Johnny. You're gonna be fine too," Jessica says, her voice cracking slightly.

"Come here," Johnny says, "come closer."

Jessica gets closer to Johnny.

> Around them, mayhem ensues.

Fire trucks.
Ambulances.
Sirens.

"What is it?" Jessica asks.

"Listen. Listen close. Everything is going to be okay. Up the road. About twenty miles. There is an exit. Exit twenty-seven. Say it."

"Say what?"

"Exit twenty-seven."

"Exit twenty-seven."

"Good. Take exit twenty-seven. Go east on Buell Road. Say it." Johnny is fading.

"East on Buell Road," she says, trying to maintain her composure.

"It intersects with Bonnet. Say Bonnet."

Jessica breaks.

She is crying.
"Bonnet."

"That's it. The money is there. In a drainage pipe under that intersection. Wait a week, then go get it."

"But the police--"

"Tell them I told you the money was in the Blazer. It burned. Tell them it's gone."

"You tell them . . ." Jessica whispers.

210

Johnny responds:

"I'm going to die."

Arty hears this. "What? Johnny? What do you mean?"

"I'm gonna die, Arty. Like Dad. I'm not coming back."

"No, Johnny. I want you to stay with me. You always take care of me--"

"It's okay, Arty. You can take care of yourself. Just do a good job for Mr. Vossen, okay? He will help you if you need it."

Arty glances down at Johnny's shirt filling up with blood.

Ambulance approaches.

He touches the shirt. The blood.

"I don't know if I can get these stains out, Johnny. But it's okay. I've got some clean clothes for you over there . . ."

"Don't worry about that, Arty. You don't have to do anything else for me. You just take care of yourself. And of Jessica. You two take care of each other . . ."

"Stay with us!" Jessica screams. "Stay with us, Johnny!"

Johnny touches her stomach.

"I am with you. I always will be . . ."

He smiles.

Jessica collapses on him.
Hugs him.
Crying.
Weeping.
"No!"

Paramedics gently pull her away from him.
"Get an IV in him."
"Got it."
"How's the vitals?"
"He's fading."

Arty is standing.
Confused.
"Is he going to be okay?"

Ignored.
Louder:
"Is he going to be okay?"

"I don't know," a paramedic snaps.

Arty watches.
They cut off Johnny's shirt.
Throw it aside.

Arty picks it up.

"I've got clean--I've got clean clothes for him. Clean clothes for him right over there. I've got clean clothes for you, Johnny. Johnny?"

Jessica hugs Arty.

He slowly puts his arms around her.

Johnny gasps.
He tries to speak.
He sees her.
She looks like an angel to him.

An angel.

Goodbye.

48

Laundromat.
   Clean.
      Organized.

   Washing machine.
      Disassembled.
         Tools.

Arty.
      Working.
              Fixing.

Jessica walks in.
   Long, light blue maternity dress.
      Showing.

"Arty!"
   "Oh," he replies, standing up. "Hi."
   He looks at her stomach and smiles.
   "Just a few more months," she says, touching her belly.

"A few more months," Arty repeats.

"What have you been doing today?" she asks.

"Collected from the dryers. Three loads of whites and six loads of darks. And working on this one."

"What's wrong with it?"

"I don't know yet. It didn't sound right. It sounded funny. And funny isn't good with a washing machine."

"Well. You wanna go get some dinner?"

"I don't think so. I've got to fix this--"

"You can fix it tomorrow. There are plenty of other machines. Put an out-of-order sign on it."

"Mr. Vossen never liked those signs."

"Arty. I keep trying to tell you. It's not Mr. Vossen's laundromat anymore. It's ours."

"Well, I don't think I like those signs either."

"Well, I don't care," Jessica says with a smile. "I'm going to make a sign and we'll hang it on there and go get something to eat. Okay?"

"I don't have any money with me."

"We've got plenty of money, Arty. Plenty. Now, lock up the office and we can go."

"Okay," Arty says, before adding, "but can

you drop me off here when we're done? I want
to finish fixing this."
"Sure."

Arty walks back.
    Locks office.
       Walks back toward Jessica.

"What are you in the mood for?" she asks.
"Mood for?"
"Yeah. To eat. What do you want to eat?"
"How about KFC?"
"No, Arty. Not again. I can't take any more
KFC. Pick something else. Anything else."
"Like what?"
"Like anything."
"Okay." Arty thinks quietly for a moment.
Then responds, "*Zalmtaart*."
"*Zalmtaart*?"
"Yes. It's Dutch. It's a pie. With salmon
and egg. I can make it."
Jessica smiles, steps out of the door, and
holds it open for Arty.
"*Zalmtaart*?" she asks.
"Yes. *Zalmtaart*."
"*Zalmtaart* it is, Arty. *Zalmtaart* it is."

Arty smiles and walks out the door.

Jessica lets the door shut.

They walk forward.

Down the street.

Happy.